Invisible

Stories

Stephen Spotte

Published by Open Books

Copyright © 2018 by Stephen Spotte

Cover image © Olga Yu/Shutterstock.com

ISBN-13: 978-1948598101

For Chuck Kinder

hillbilly poet, novelist, and last mountain dancer

Contents

Acknowledgements

"Blue Unicorn," "Old Woman Framed and Backlit," "The Sometime Bass with the Goodly Set," and "Home is the Sailor, Under the Sea" appeared previously in *Home is the Sailor, Under the Sea: Mermaid Stories*; "Partly Sunny (or Cloudy)," "An Old Man with Big Hands," Hatchery Life," Fat Dreams," and "Batness" were published previously in *An Optimist in Hell: Stories*; "Invisible" originally appeared in *Litscapes: Collected US Writings 2015*.

Life is a web weaving a spider.

Mia Couto, "The Ex-future Priest and His Would-be Widow"

Invisible

I DON'T WONDER WHAT I am or where I might be headed, and I never look back. That's seeing yourself too clearly, the mistakes and trouble everywhere. Better to leave it behind.

It's nice here in the barn watching sunlight slip through cracks in the old boards, throwing imaginary animals onto shadow.

About head-high there's a knot hole shaped like a rabbit. When I was little—eight or nine—I'd come out here on summer afternoons and sit in the hay with my back against the splinters waiting for that rabbit to show itself. I'd stare and stare at the far wall, not once looking up at the knot hole, and suddenly, like magic, there was the rabbit.

As the sun moved lower the rabbit dimmed and faded away. They all laughed at me, but I could never shoot a rabbit. Squirrels are different.

The light glows purple and fades as another day goes by. Through board cracks the trunks of the trees turn soft. I'm grown now with no time for shadow rabbits.

Starting in fall there's heifers to feed, and the mules need their hay pitched too. They work all the seasons, these mules, but in fall and winter there's nothing for them except pulling logs out of the woods. Not a bad life if you ask me. I can think of worse things than being born a mule. Being invisible is a lot worse.

Outside the leaves are turning colors. It's their time. I like watching them through the big doors we keep propped open to let in air. I like it when the wind hurries them down, leaving behind a space where a leaf once grew. Not an empty space, but a space filled with emptiness. Tunnels. Every leaf-hole connected to another, the bunch of them twisting and turning away like memories.

I dip into the sweet-grain and give each mule a taste. They see me head for the bag and perk up their ears, stamp a heavy sound.

Can they know what's underneath? Their hooves leave flat places on the floors of the stalls. The hoof prints cover up others already there, making them disappear at the edges like days layering on.

With time the floors slope to the middle. Then I rake out the stalls and fetch the wheelbarrow. I fill in the depressions with fresh clay, dusty pale as dry cement. I breathe in its lightness as I shovel. My snot turns white. The stuff blows against me, mats my hair, turns me into a different kind of invisible. So big, and all that happiness in a handful of sweet-grain. There's worse things to be born than a mule.

The heifers look up as I fork their hay, eyes big and trusting like Mary Louise's. Hers were blue. Big as a heifer's and blue.

She cried last time and told me love is all two people need. We could see it through, the bunch of us, her kin and mine. She pressed her face against my neck. Tears trickled down my skin like hot sweat.

Love can do that, mix the hard with the easy until problems seem harmless. I know better. I come out of the shadows, trouble starts. It always did and always will. Stay in the greenbriers like a rabbit, that's what I say. Mary Louise never understood, and I couldn't tell her. Now it's over and done. Never look back . . . but it's hard sometimes.

Pap hobbles through the big doors looking dark against the last light. I can't see his face at first and think how he could be anybody, even a scarecrow with that old straw hat and coveralls. He drags one leg; the arm on the same side hangs flopping with every step. He's got a cane now. I made it for him out of hickory. The bottom is brown from manure, the top brown from the sweat and dirt of his hand, but the middle still shines gray.

He nods and heads for the tractor where his parts and tools are spread out on the seat and on the empty hay cart hooked up behind. Pap hasn't done farm work since the stroke, but he intends to tune that tractor engine before spring. He can't talk now. He's got one arm and one leg for a job that needs two of both. I nod back.

Pap gets mad if we talk to him now that he can't answer. It bothers the others. Not me. I'd rather not talk anyway. Pap has made it plain we're to stay the hell away from the tractor.

Pap's invisible too. We all are. Our births aren't recorded, so it's as if we were never born. Sometimes I see my reflection in a store window and think, there goes a ghost, but ghosts were somebody once. A ghost leaves behind a record of a life. Paperwork filed with a name and address, next of kin, accomplishments.

I finish up the heifers, get the milk buckets, and go to the end of the barn to milk the two cows. The barn cats hear the buckets clang and come tumbling out of the haymow. I empty some ants and bits of hay from their bowl. They live on milk and mice and whatever else they catch, a bird or a chipmunk. I sometimes find the evidence: feathers and bits of fur mixed in with the hay. Our cats are born and grow up here. Some stay. Others go off and don't come back. When one leaves another takes its place. We're never without cats.

As I stoop to pet them I think how they're invisible too. They have no history either, like the leaves and the light, a different light today than yesterday, a different light every day since the world started.

Nobody knows our situation except kin and people who marry in. I tried explaining it to Mary Louise. Now that's over and done.

We barter produce and make some cash cutting wood. We don't pay taxes or Social Security. There's no electric bill. None of us has ever set foot inside a schoolhouse or had a driver's license, but we drive our pickup over every inch of road in this county because Pap's third cousin is sheriff. The county is plenty big enough for me. I never had the urge to go anyplace else, until now.

The spiders are starting to hide away for winter. Maybe they live under boards or in hay. I don't know. I see those brown spiders come out in spring, each to its own corner. A spider lays a big ball of eggs and hangs there, never moving. More patience than I'll ever have. Sometimes I drop in a fly and watch while the spider kills it and wraps it up in spider silk, a little blanket of death. Not quite the same situation, I'm thinking, but the dead are still dead.

The mules stamp. If I was superstitious I might think they could read my mind. They can't. They're just mules wanting sweet-grain and wondering what I'm doing down here at the other end of the barn.

Pap is hammering on that rusty engine casing. I hear him breathing long and hoarse. I can tell he's mad, the hammer's heavy. His mechanic's light throws a bright circle on the floor. Maybe his lungs will bust open. I don't think he cares anymore. Now that he can't talk. Only he and I know the truth. Not even his third cousin knows. Kin are kin, but close kin count more.

I tried explaining things to Mary Louise. I asked her to sit down and watch the rabbit come up on the wall, but she was yelling at me and crying. All I said was we couldn't get married. She kept asking why and hitting me with her fists. I couldn't tell her why: invisible is forever.

She wanted something else. She said we could go to Charleston where people don't know us. I could find work. Be among strangers? When you're invisible, it's the strangers who are dangerous. They might tell, and suddenly your picture's in the paper.

Picture. I'll never stop seeing that one blaze up behind my eyes, a red desert of washboard dunes. A picture memorized out of a magazine when I lay with a fever long ago.

After I got well I went looking. I found it, crumpled up and smeared with ashes. Pap smoothed it out. The land of Egypt, he said, where Pharaoh persecuted the Israelites, and when he opened the coal stove the flames licked it out of his fingers.

Why that came to mind just then I couldn't say, but I felt the purity of fire again. White heat behind my eyes.

God's anger.

When my eyesight came back everything was like before. The same but somehow different. There were boards all around, stalls with their dug floors, light coming in through the big doors. The rabbit.

Who died in anger?

To be consumed in fire when the leaves are turning makes a certain sense: red leaves, red desert, no green anywhere. Then the chill of the hollows, of darkness out beyond. The valley of the shadow of death.

I saw what I'd done. Shadows without walls. The sudden stillness was God's whispered forgiveness. In the desert everything moves with the wind, dunes gliding over dunes. Pharaoh's army lies buried under sand. Pap told us so.

Here the boards resist. I'm safe from being covered over.

The mules hear something. They stop and listen, ears toggling. Mules can tell what's down there compacting slowly in the quiet.

I'm glad those stalls are done. Someday I can stop thinking about it. Never look back, that's the secret. Pap came in just as I was finishing up, but he knew. He stopped and looked at me, and his eyes didn't say a thing.

In summer, the daylight slides into evening. Time is gradual; there's a softness. Now the difference is a thin pale sheet. Mary Louise's kin will wonder.

When the moon comes up I'll start walking toward it. There won't be anything behind me, not even a shadow.

Maud and Mad

WHEN MAUD FIRST SAW the ghost it was sitting on the toilet complaining. Although its words were mostly inaudible the tone was unmistakably Henry's. Putting these facts together she concluded it must be Henry's ghost. Satisfied, she continued past the bathroom and sat down heavily in her chair by the window. That wouldn't do and she knew it. With a groan she stuffed feet into slippers, got up from the chair, and shuffled to the bathroom just to be sure. The complaining grew louder. She returned to the chair to get her glasses before taking another look. It was Henry's ghost alright because when it saw Maud it said goddammit where's Jimmy Smo's medicine, can't you see I'm suffering?

That was how long ago now? Weeks? Months? Who could remember. Time didn't exactly whiz by here at the sick home. Sometimes it was tough to know who was crazier, her or Henry's ghost. When she tells the nurses she needs another bathroom to use because Henry's ghost is always on the toilet and is she supposed to sit on it or something and they smile and say sure dearie we understand now go use your own bathroom and stop bothering the other patients to use theirs. So what can she do except sit down on Henry's ghost and pee right through it although if the truth be told it never seemed to notice.

Then she announces she is hiking down to the drugstore to get medicine for Jimmy Smo. That used to be the name of Henry's hemorrhoid before he died, Henry. They look at each other like she must be crazy, the nurses. *Me* crazy she thinks? It wasn't me picked that name for a hemorrhoid it was Henry's idea. But they won't let her out and she goes back and asks Henry's ghost if a ghost hemorrhoid hurts the same as a live person's and whether a ghost can feel pain and it replies don't ask me go ask a ghost and what a stupid question.

One day she asks Henry's ghost what color are the walls of the bathroom and it says pink like always. Then she asks it where it's sitting at the moment, not the toilet but which apartment, and it answers Brighton Beach, Brooklyn, where I been thirty-nine years. And as proof it reminds her that he Henry had never wished to travel because Brighton Beach has everything a person could want so why go anywhere. She remembers the time they talked about Florida but Henry lost interest when the travel agent tells him it's more than a thousand miles, Florida. Henry's smart-mouth brothers teased him Henry you don't need a passport to leave Brooklyn as if Henry is afraid he can't find Florida or maybe afraid he can't find his way back.

Then Maud tells Henry's ghost this is the sick home where Maddie and Frankie put me, where everyone is senile or has the alls himer disease or worse, where we're drooling ourselves to death. You who don't know from nothing about sick homes. You never had the pleasure considering you died instead. All we do here is look out the window or maybe go outside to feed the squirrels. The address, it's Ocean Parkway not Brighton First Road and Boardwalk. And the walls, Henry, the walls are green. This bathroom has green walls. And Henry's ghost replies why would anyone feed squirrels they're just rats with fluffy tails and only an idiot would feed a rat. And besides I know pink from green and these walls are pink and if this is Ocean Parkway how did I get here, and Maud has to admit it's a good question.

She remembers as a girl going into the bathroom on Sunday mornings pretending she needs to look in the mirror, Henry on the toilet. Henry the kidder. Hey, you're standing on the comics you silly broad, and he'd run his hand up her leg. It's a game they played. Maud squealed, Henry chuckled. Hey Legs, Henry's ghost says today, there's no goddamn newspaper in this joint where you claim you moved? A man can't take a crap without the sports pages. Tell me again why'd you pick Ocean Parkway, or so you say. She waits for the cold touch, any touch, but nothing happens. Maybe ghosts didn't have hands a live person could feel.

Her ankles ached. She bent over stiffly and examined them. They were swollen from not being elevated. What legs she had as a girl! In fact the first thing Henry ever said to her is hi Legs. Henry spots her on the boardwalk where her and Mad are having sodas at Nathan's Finest. Man, Henry says he'd said to himself, now there is one great pair of legs. Got to meet the gal that goes with 'em. And he had, and so handsome in his army uniform! Private First Class Henry Cohen at your service ma'am. Home on leave after single-handedly protecting America and your own personal gorgeous legs from Hitler. Yes indeed you owe it all to me and to show your gratitude I'm buying you and your friend another soda. After all, ladies, you can't be too grateful. Who could resist talk like that? Her and Mad laughed themselves sick. That Henry, what a kidder.

Maud settled her ankles onto the footstool and leaned back with a sigh. Those were the days. Summer of '46. Her and Henry courting, strolling the boardwalk in the sea air, laughing with friends, stopping at the little stands to buy sodas and knishes, Henry insisting they ride the Cyclone every night even when she doesn't want to. It's the thrill, Henry would argue, it gets the blood pumping, makes you feel alive. But the real reason is so she can pretend to be afraid and not notice when Henry puts his hand on her knee. It was harmless enough. If that's what it took to keep a man, so what? And Mad agreed. When she told Mad about it Mad only wrinkled her nose and said, Maud if you don't want Henry just say the word because he can take me up on that roller coaster and put his hand halfway between my knee and you-know-where anytime he likes and they laughed until they cried.

God she missed Mad. More than her dead parents, sometimes more even than Henry. Some twosome they were that summer of '46, Mad short and blonde and real curvaceous, Maud slender and dark and leggy. The boardwalk was their promenade and when they sashayed past Nathan's Finest you could have heard the wolf whistles all the way to West Eighth Street. Mad and Maud, Maud and Mad. Everyone on the boardwalk knew them. They were—what was Henry's word—*infamous*. And military fellas everywhere all so handsome in their uniforms. What choice did they have, Mad and Maud? It was practically their patriotic duty to smile back. They told each other all the time if it wasn't for the war they'd have nothing to do with these fellas, especially since hardly any of them came from Coney Island or even Brooklyn. They wanted to tell you how brave they were in the fighting and some God forbid wanted you to look at their wounds! Can you believe it? But she'd said to Mad, I'll take Henry thank you. Henry who spent his hitch as a clerk-typist at Fort Dix over in Jersey. When fellas shipped to the European Theater or the Pacific Theater it was Henry typed their orders and afterward he went to the movies.

They got married soon after Henry's discharge from the army and moved to a cold-water flat in Brighton Beach. It had two rooms and Maud heated water in a tea kettle for baths. The view was an alley filled with garbage cans, the curtains cut from some old cloth donated by Momma Irene, Henry's mother. But it was perfect for the two of them. One day her ma comes to visit. They're having coffee and her ma says Maud you should clean those windows and Maud says what for and her ma says see the floor it looks dirty and Maud says I cleaned the floor but I see what you mean and her ma says it's the light coming through the windows and dirty windows make the light dirty which makes the floor look dirty. That afternoon she gets a bucket of hot water and vinegar and washes and polishes those windows until they shine and when Henry comes home he says what happened the place is so clean did we move when I'm not looking or what.

Henry was lucky. He didn't have to find a job after he got out the Army because he had one waiting for him in Poppa Abe's men's store over in Flatbush. Henry and his smart-mouth brothers were salesmen, fellas that lean on suit racks wearing big toothy smiles and measuring tapes around their necks. For about the first ten years they worked the floor. Only Poppa Abe was allowed to measure the customers. This was the personal touch. This was why the customers came back and if you didn't believe it you better not ask because Poppa Abe would bend your ear for an hour. Poppa Abe's uncle from the old country was the tailor, but he stayed in the back room with the sewing machine and needles and other stuff tailors use.

The name on the store was Abe Cohen's Fine Clothes for Men. Poppa Abe had the sign repainted about every two years so it never looked shabby. A shabby sign is low-class and drives away the customers he said. The store was full of customers all the time because Poppa Abe believed it pays to advertise. His ads said Abe Cohen's Fine Clothes for Men, We Cater to the Professional and Working Man A Like, and the ads had drawings of tall slender men leaning against lamp posts with cigarettes dangling off their lips. These men had moustaches and fedoras pulled down over their eyes which made them look very mysterious. Henry said it's because Poppa Abe was short and dumpy and he himself had always wanted to look like Walter Pidgeon.

The store made a good living for the whole family. Henry and his smart-mouth brothers eventually were allowed to measure the customers too and it made them feel important and even though Maud thought the whole thing seemed stupid she kept her mouth shut. No sense killing a golden goose that lays grade-A eggs she told herself. In '52 they moved to a high rise in Brighton Beach with a view of the boardwalk and stayed thirty-nine years. It was a spectacular apartment, two bedrooms, a kitchen, a bathroom, a combination dining room-living room. A dream apartment. And the next year little Maddie was born.

Naturally she named her daughter Madelene. When Mad visited her in the maternity ward and Maud told her the baby's name she said you mean this beautiful child is named after *me*? You named her after *me*? And so on and when Maud said sure why not and didn't I do a good job keeping the secret they both started sniffling and pretty soon the faucets turned on and they were hugging each other and honking on hankies and it got so loud the nurses ran in and asked was something wrong and is there an emergency.

Mad of course married Lenny about a year after Maud and Henry sewed the button on, as Poppa Abe put it. Lenny was good to her but he was kind of a sourpuss, always carping about Mad's cooking and housekeeping and it wasn't like she didn't try. Lenny was a kosher butcher and came home all covered with dried blood and stuff and when Maud asked how could she stand it Mad wrinkled her nose and said it's no worse than having your period except Lenny has his every day but Saturday. Boy was that a hoot! Their sides had finally stopped aching when Lenny comes home and says he's out of clean aprons at the shop and can Mad maybe wash a couple for him that night and that starts the hooting all over again and Lenny is asking what did I say and what's so goddamn funny.

About '56 Henry discovered it, the hemorrhoid, and let out a scream that Maud heard through two closed doors. At the time she is standing in the hall talking to Mrs. Goldstein from apartment seven-oh-eight who is wondering if her husband can maybe get a discount on clothes and Maud asks is he in the union because Cohen's gives a discount to union fellas and Mrs. Goldstein scratches her neck and says she doesn't think so unless there's an accounting union.

Sonofabitch that hurts yells Henry from behind the bathroom door and Maud runs into their apartment wondering if it's a heart attack or he cut himself changing a light bulb. Henry was never too handy around the house. By now the baby is awake and screaming, but Maud and Henry are standing over the toilet bowl looking at the bloody water. They must have stood there a long time because the kid eventually shouted herself out.

Henry named his hemorrhoid right there and then. He called it Jimmy Smolinski after a Polish kid in his junior high. Naturally he tells the whole family about it, Momma Irene and Poppa Abe, his smart-mouth brothers, Mad and Lenny, and anyone else who would listen. Maud's ma and pop had already died so they weren't around to tell.

Why Jimmy Smolinski everyone asked. Because, said Henry, Jimmy Smolinski was the craziest kid in school. He acted so crazy we used to tell him Jimmy you got a hemorrhoid for a brain and everyone laughed except Momma Irene who thought the story was low-class. Later of course Maddie found out about Henry's hemor-rhoid named Jimmy Smolinski or Jimmy Smo for short and natu-rally Frankie too and probably everyone in Flatbush who came into the store knew about Henry's hemorrhoid.

When Henry needed hemorrhoid medicine he would say Legs don't forget the medicine for Jimmy Smo and he was very peculiar about what medicine it was. He always used Preparation H and not anything else. Brand loyalty he said. It's what makes the world go around, he said. Why, everyone has brand loyalty and Maud had to admit she did too. Always buying Tide to wash the clothes, Ivory Soap to wash the baby. Look at Poppa Abe says Henry, he has always been loyal to Lincolns and when Maud mentions that Poppa Abe has never owned a car or even had a driving license Henry says so what because if Poppa Abe ever gets a driving license and buys a car it will be a Lincoln no doubt about it.

Theirs had been a good marriage, better than Mad's, better than Maddie's. Evenings during the years when Maddie was still little were best. They could hear Henry's key in the lock and Maddie would run to greet him and then the stories started. What an excit-ing job, Henry! Like an astronaut or something. One time he walks in, announces Legs line up the kid this is a good one. Henry always liked Maddie there when he told stories. She sat on the floor real quiet and her eyes got big and Maud guessed she herself acted like that too except she sat in a chair.

Anyway Henry comes in all excited and says he should get salesman of the year for the job he pulled off today. This fella comes in the store all dirty says he needs a shirt, couple pairs of skivvies. Henry flashes the ivories and asks him you union be-cause Cohen's always has special deals for union fellas, like anoth-er 10% off the stuff on sale for 30% off, and then he adds just for our benefit, and what do they know, the store still knocks down 85% profit. Fella says yeah, sanitation worker. Henry says what's the occasion, fella says he's taking her to dinner first time, his girl. Henry says your best girl, right? Want to really impress her, right? Fella says yeah. Then Henry asks him his name. He says it's Vinnie something a last name only another wop could pronounce.

Henry says to the fella lookit you need more'n a shirt, new skivvies. You need a new jacket too. This girl's got class I can tell; she's gonna think you're cheap, know what I mean. The fella says yeah, but he's not so sure. Henry drags him to a rack and says feel the cloth on this jacket. The fella reaches out and touches it real careful like he's petting a dead cat. He asks how much, Henry tells him. Henry slips the jacket on the fella and calls, oh Mr. Cohen could you help us please. Henry and his smart-mouth brothers always referred to him in the store as Mr. Cohen, Poppa Abe, because it sounded classier than yelling hey Pop.

Poppa Abe he knows a fish when he sees one. He comes running, measures the fella, fusses over him, says he looks terrific and the alterations are free. Then Henry asks you got slacks. The fella says yeah. Henry asks what color, the fella says brown. Henry gasps a little, maybe staggers back to show he's stunned. *Brown* he says? You're gonna wear *brown* with this nice gray jacket? Let me tell you Vinnie, brown won't hack it. Now look over these charcoal jobs here. Poppa Cohen, he knows his cue. He comes at a trot the tape stretched out in front of him and before the fella can inhale he's being measured crotch to shoe tops.

Now, Henry says, we got skivvies, jacket, slacks. You need a shirt, socks, and shoes. But I got all them already except the shirt, the fella says. Henry closes his eyes and waggles his index finger in the air like he does sometimes with Maddie when she's whining. Vinnie you gotta trust me says Henry. The next thing one of Henry's smart-mouth brothers is fitting the guy for black calfskins and whipping a couple pairs of socks on top of the pile while the other brother picks out a shirt. Oh, Henry says, we almost forgot the belt. The fella says he's got a belt, he's wearing it. Henry looks horrified. You mean the belt you wear on the sanitation truck Vinnie? *That* belt? You're squeezing my onions, right? And he whips a nice leather job onto the pile.

Henry totes up the bill, the fella looks at it and says I can give you thirty bucks now the rest tomorrow. Henry tells him that's fine, pockets the thirty. To quote Henry, the fella says he ain't got but thirty bucks, you know how they mangle the English language them wops from Flatbush.

Then Henry puts his head close to this fella's and says Vinnie these clothes are gonna get you laid, guaranteed. And if the worse should happen and you don't get laid, future alterations are free. But this deal is just between us. Don't say nothing to old Mr. C or them two hairballs leaning on the clothes rack. Got it? The fella nods like he's got it and walks out the store happy as a clam. Course he don't know that at Cohen's all alterations are free all the time.

Maud especially remembers what follows. Now Henry spreads his feet, opens his arms, throws back his head like he's Frank Sinatra just finished singing "Moon Over Miami" in front of about a million people and suddenly they're clapping and screaming. And Maud can see the picture in her mind clear as anything. Maddie is two maybe three and her and Maud jump up and they're clapping and yelling Yea Daddy and Yea Henry and he swoops down and hugs them so hard he stops their breath.

That kind of stuff happened a lot. Maud remembered exactly when it hit her why her and Henry were so happy together. They're at the Parkway bowling one night and Mad and Lenny are scrapping as usual. Maud's sitting there listening to them and watching balls roll down the alleys and suddenly she feels all electric like a person feels when they guess the answer to an important question they been asking all their life but didn't really know it. It was like a smack across the chops with a dead carp. Their lives are two separate balls rolling down separate alleys at different speeds, Mad and Lenny's. Her and Henry's life is one ball rolling down one alley. In other words, Maud thinks to herself, a woman wants security with a man, kids, nice place to live. But more important she wants to be included in his life. Just be included, that's all. So she jumps out the chair and gives Henry a hug and says I love you so much and he says I love you too Legs now step up to the plate and roll your line good 'cause he's looking to cream us tonight, Lenny. And she grabs that ball and sticks her fingers in the holes and can't remember when she's been so happy.

One evening, it's a few months before Henry has the heart attack and dies, everyone has got together at their apartment for drinks before going out to dinner: Mad and Lenny, Maddie and Frankie, and of course Maud and Henry. The liquor is as they say flowing freely and Henry is in fine form. He's telling about the day Maddie comes home from work says she's in love with this Italian kid from Sheepshead Bay who turns out to be Frankie. He went to college, Maddie gushes, and he's an accountant like Mrs. Goldstein's husband in seven-oh-eight and all the time Henry is impersonating Maddie and he's got her down perfect even to talking with her hands and all, Maddie.

We're saying that's nice Maddie, Henry goes on, and are you serious and she says that he's asked her to marry him and she said yes even though she's known him only a couple weeks, Frankie. And Maud is saying I don't know Maddie he isn't Jewish and Henry says so what at least he's not a stump jumper from Kentucky like a kid he knew in the army.

This kid's name is Abe Peck and he's just got to Fort Dix in Jersey and Henry says hello I'm Henry and he says hi I'm Abe and Henry says my pop's name is Abe and Henry's thinking that because Abe is a Jewish name this kid Abe Peck must be a Jew. So he asks where do you go to synagogue. Abe Peck says syna-*what* and Henry says, you know, church. And the kicker is, says Henry, this Abe Peck has never seen a Jew before and thinks hillbillies from Kentucky are God's chosen people as if God could even find Kentucky for chrissakes.

But he has religion of some kind and was baptized, Abe Peck. He says they did it to him in a creek with a bunch of other people and the reverend told them this creek is filled with holy water so they all start moaning and splashing around and he dunks each one, the reverend. Now this creek has a hundred or so shithouses hanging over the bank and the place gets a good flush about once a year when it floods. So Henry he asks this Abe Peck, hey Abe was you baptized before or after the flood and Abe Peck says he don't remember but what does it matter and Henry says he thinks it would make a difference whether you come up for air with a soggy page of the Sears catalog stuck to your head.

By Maud's recollection her and Mad are laughing hysterically and Lenny, Maddie, and Frankie are probably wishing they can go eat Chinese without these three. So they waltz out to the elevator together and who should be there when they get in but Mrs. Silberman from eighth floor with some of her relatives visiting from Queens. And when they're all packed inside like smoked herrings and the doors close Mrs. Silberman says to her relatives these are my neighbors the Cohens from seventh floor and their friends and this is their daughter Maddie and her husband Frankie. Then she lowers her voice so nobody can hear except everyone in the elevator and adds and he's a gentile, Frankie.

Nice hat Mrs. Silberman, says Henry, although I never seen a purple ostrich feather on one before, on a pork-pie I mean. And he says it just loud enough so nobody can hear except everyone in the elevator. Mad she's squished against the back but Maud sees her nose wrinkle and that's the sign of a big laugh on the way. And sure enough she's trying to choke it back, trying to hold it until Mrs. Silberman maybe gets off the elevator but the elevator is still going down. Lenny gives her a look like he's going to clamp his hand over her mouth any minute but then the hooting starts and Maud's got no choice except to hoot some herself. Henry is grinning like the Chesterfield cat, Lenny and Frankie pretend they don't know from nothing, and Maddie turns red as that awful pasta sauce he makes her cook, Frankie. Some incident that was! Mad and Maud talked about it for weeks and even the mention of it started them hooting all over again.

Half the laughter stopped when Henry died and the other half went with Mad when she died a year later. The cancer took her, Mad, and in the end she looked like one of those inmates from the death camps during the war, walking cadavers with numbers tattooed on their arms and eyes big and empty and soulful. Lenny was left and of course Maddie and Frankie but none of them liked to laugh.

When Mad's pain got bad Maud took to visiting her every day. He behaved like a jerk up to the end, Lenny, still going out nights to play cards and carping at Mad to clean up the apartment. One night he goes out and Maud is there and she says Mad let me clean up the place so he'll stop badgering you, Lenny. But Mad says forget it, come sit beside me on the bed. And her eyes fill up with tears and she says that without her, meaning Maud, she could not have stood it. Maud looks into those eyes and they seem to grow into deep pools of blue water and she is thinking funny how a few teardrops can make the eyes seem so much bigger like the tears magnify them or something. And then they're holding onto each other like one of them might suddenly be yanked away and Mad says how much like a sister Maud has been all her life and how important especially since she never had kids, Mad. Then she pushes Maud away and starts dabbing her eyes and says now let's not get maudlin and Maud always remembered that. What a twosome, Madelene and Maudlin. Maudlin and Madelene.

Then one day Maddie and Frankie call a family meeting and tell her Momma you can't stay where you lived most of your life, the apartment, because you're going senile and needing aftercare. So what's aftercare Maud had said. It sounds to me like who cares after I'm dead. And they said no it isn't the same, just a bunch of strangers to help her when she doesn't want to be helped, to be there when she wants to be alone. It's a wonderful opportunity to live in a gentle, park-like setting as it said on this brochure for the sick home on Ocean Parkway even though everyone knew parks are for bums and pigeons.

Maud groaned and lifted her feet off the footstool. Maybe women remember the happy times best because they're always cleaning up after everyone else. Drying eyes, wiping noses, sponging up barf. What did she need that for at her age? Why dry her own eyes and wipe her own nose when it means getting up from the chair and going to the bathroom and arm-wrestling Henry's ghost for a length of toilet paper and listening to the complaining. Better to remember the good times, the laughter.

"Momma, you okay?" It was Maddie. What was she doing here?

"How long you been here Maddie?"

"About an hour. You been talking to yourself, babbling on about Daddy and Aunt Mad and dirty windows and the times you had when you was young, and laughing and crying sometimes. You okay?

18

I got to go home and make Frankie's supper. You need anything?"

"I need some Preparation H next time you come."

"You having a problem Momma? I mean, you constipated?"

"Course not Maddie. You know I been regular as church bells all my life. It's for your father. And be sure it's Preparation H and not some other medicine for Jimmy Smo. Remember your father's brand loyalty."

Later when Maddie's cooking supper with Frankie in the other room in front of the television she yells, "I'm worried Frankie. She's talking to herself, Momma. She wants me to bring some medicine for Jimmy Smo next week like Daddy's there with her."

"Jimmy Smo," snorts Frankie surfing through the channels. "Your pop for chrissakes is the only guy I know who names his hemorrhoid like it's a little poodle or something for chrissakes."

"Frankie will you go with me to see Momma next week?" She waits for an answer but Tim McCarver's voice from the television tells her it's too late. He's found the Mets game on WOR channel 9 and vanished into the crowd, Frankie.

The Fattest
First Hypothesis

IT HAPPENED ON THE fifth day of their collective rebirth and metamorphosis as sailors. The Priest said that the timing had religious
significance and quoted by memory a passage from the Book of
Genesis, something about God having created the great whales and
the waters bringing forth abundantly. Previously creatures of sidewalks and city parks, they were now a minor component of the sea's
flotsam, "mere drifting plankton" in the words of the Scientist. The
raft had unfortunately sprung some new leaks. According to the
Engineer, who had just that moment completed a survey, they were
up Shit Creek almost to the headwaters. Faced with the prospect of
sinking, their lack of a paddle was hardly relevant.

What happened was Amir had deserted. Amir, who belonged to
a distant sect of the Brashnevists in coastal Zykrisikistan, a place of
excessive aridity populated by worshippers of stones in whose lat-
ticed interiors were thought to reside the only true gods, creators of
the universe. Not too far-fetched, mused the Scientist upon hearing
Amir's timid admission. He was thinking of the fist-sized ball of
matter that had exploded, rocketed outward to form the present
universe, and was expanding still. He mentioned his geodes, which
he had personally wrenched from the earth and sawn in half to ex-

pose their crystalline interiors. Amir's sensitive face convulsed at the sacrilege. Stones? The Engineer squeezed her brows together. Useful as a matrix for concrete. Good for road beds. But when the Priest had called Amir's religion blasphemous and shaken his cross at him, this devout believer in the holiness of all that is mineral jumped overboard. Being a strong swimmer, he soon was lost between the swells and eventually disappeared over the horizon.

"At least the raft will ride higher in the water," said the Engineer.

The Scientist rolled his eyes upward, the better to calculate how much drinking water would be saved for the rest of them. "Two swallows each per day," he proclaimed proudly.

"Poor Amir, child of God. He shall be in my prayers tonight. Jesus cherished the Heathen," said the Priest. But he was secretly glad to be rid of the nonbeliever, and if his companions showed no inclination to embrace Christ, at least they weren't foreigners.

Six days previously their caïque had sunk in the middle of the Argolopterian Sea, casting them adrift without so much as an onion or slice of melon for sustenance. Their water might last another week, but no longer. The nearest atoll was far to the west. Unless a ship happened by, they were doomed.

They rode in silence up one side of a swell and down the other, sometimes sideways, sometimes at an angle, occasionally forward or backward. At the Engineer's insistence they had arranged themselves in the shape of an equilateral triangle, the better to balance the raft.

"We are in God's hands," intoned the Priest. He was corpulent from many church suppers and the cakes and pies left on his doorstep by doting women of his parish. His red nose veins glistened in the sun. "I wish we had some wine," he said, then added quickly, "so that I could perform the Sacrament of the Eucharist."

"Actually, we are in the hands of our own physiologies," replied the Scientist. He was enormously fat from sitting motionless in front of a computer screen and eating chrysalis chips. "If we can get by on a few swallows of water each day and catch a fish besides, we might not perish. I wish we had beer," he added, "although beer is a diuretic."

"If you want the truth, we are in the hands of DuPont Corporation," said the Engineer. "DuPont built this raft, and if the glue and stitching hold together we might survive long enough to drift across a shipping lane and be rescued." The Engineer was very fat as a result of her involvement with AA (Anorexia Anonymous), whose mission it was to coax young girls into ingesting a daily minimum of eight thousand kilocalories.

They listened to the water rumble underneath them and go hissing past their ears. "We must get our house in order," said the Engineer with determination. "It's now or never." She often spoke in platitudes on the assumption that slogans made her seem decisive to others.

"We are all tenants in God's house," said the Priest. He looked at the sea turning burgundy under the setting sun and prayed silently for a bottle of Madeira.

"We should be quiet and sleep," the Scientist said. "Talking increases the amount of water vapor lost from the mouth, and quiescence maintains the body's metabolism at resting level so that less water is required to carry out the normal oxidative processes." They closed their eyes and slept spread-eagled to keep from rolling over, their feet sometimes touching on the raft's slippery, undulating floor. In the night a Barkelonian flying trout landed among them.

"A gift from God!" exclaimed the Priest upon awakening and seeing the fish. It was quite large, measuring perhaps eighteen dentimes from nose to tail. Its sides were silvery with azure and vermilion markings in a Penrose tiling design. "How sad that we have no means of preparing it. And sadder still, we have no chilled chardonnay." The Priest gazed heavenward and made the sign of the cross.

The Scientist struggled up on one elbow, balancing himself by planting his other elbow against the side of the raft. "Cooking it would waste the liquid it contains," he said. "The blood and tissues of saltwater fishes are about one-third the saltiness of seawater. We must suck the juices out of this specimen and gain its water."

Upon hearing this the Engineer's upper lip tried desperately to displace her nose. "Death by dehydration is preferable to sucking on a raw fish," she replied. "Maybe I can devise an appropriate tool." And she did, taking a large garlic press from the emergency survival kit and filing off its projections so that juices from the fish could be squeezed into a drinking glass. They passed the glass among them and drank its foul contents.

The Engineer was about to toss the remains of the fish overboard when the Scientist raised his hand. "Wait! Perhaps we can use this fish to catch another." He rummaged in the emergency survival kit and extracted a fish hook and length of twine. He baited the hook and lowered it overboard. Almost immediately there was a tug, and the Scientist pulled in a flopping Barkelonian flying trout. This specimen was smaller than the first, measuring perhaps twelve dentimes. The Scientist cut the fish into strips, which they rolled up and ate as sushi.

"That actually was pretty decent," proclaimed the Engineer, smacking her lips appreciatively. "For the first time in a week I don't feel hungry."

"Excellent indeed," agreed the Priest, "although an icy Chablis would have been the perfect accompaniment."

"Is wine all you think about?" asked the Engineer.

"Certainly not!" answered the Priest, feeling insulted. "However, images of wine are traditional in the great literature of sailors cast adrift. Consider Coleridge's *The Rime of the Ancient Mariner*," and he quoted,

> *Alone, alone, all, all alone,*
> *Alone on a wine-dark sea!*
> *And never a saint took pity*
> *On my soul in agony.*

The Engineer licked her fingers and leaned back against the side of the raft. "I believe the line is, "Alone on a *wide wide* sea." The Priest looked doubtful but made no protest.

And so they drifted, day after day. The sun scalded them from above, and at night the chill of the sea entered their bones through the writhing floor of the raft. But they were neither thirsty nor hungry because every day the Scientist caught a fish using as bait the remains of the fish caught the previous day. In fact, their lives improved in several ways.

Using the Priest's cassock, amice, alb, and cincture, the Engineer devised a sun shelter to shade them during the heat of the day. With scissors from the emergency survival kit, she made thin blankets by cutting their clothes (including the Priest's chasuble and stole) into strips and sewing the strips together with shoelaces, after first removing the aglets. Their shoes had become soggy and useless, and besides, not much walking gets done aboard a life raft.

The Scientist, in addition to catching fish, became the preparer of their food. With the Engineer's assistance, he learned to squeeze juices from floating seaweed. The liquid obtained was placed in the sun to ferment. To the Priest's delight, the end product was an amber wine with a slight aftertaste of iodine, not at all unpleasant. Once they caught a fat gawklet on the fishing line. They removed its feathers and cooked it using sunlight focused through a magnifying glass.

The underside of the raft became a smorgasbord of edible marine life: succulent barnacles, mussels, sea anemones, and bryozoans grown fat on invisible plankton; chitins and periwinkles stuffed with diatoms; sea lettuce that was soft and emerald green. They had only to reach under the raft to gather enough for a fragrant bouillabaisse. Wine and drinking water were no longer luxuries. Both now poured freely from solar-powered stills assembled by the Engineer using lengths of fuel line, several spare fuel cans, and solar batteries from the emergency survival kit. In all, they were happy and contented. The hardships of their early days at sea became a distant memory, and they no longer yearned to be rescued.

The days turned to weeks, the weeks melted into months. They drifted in a slow southwest gyre, seeing only the peaks and troughs of swells around them and the sky above. They were tanned and even fatter than before. Their feet had become soft and pasty.

One morning they sighted a bright red object on the horizon. It was the size of a soccer ball and seemed to be moving toward them. The object disappeared momentarily in the nadir of a swell, then reappeared on a crest. They were now too fat to stand and could do nothing except watch it rise and fall before them. At last they were close enough to see it clearly.

"It's Amir!" cried the Engineer, who had the sharpest eyes. Indeed it was, and still wearing his red swim cap. Upon seeing them, Amir began to stroke rapidly away employing a modified Zykrisikistantinian crawl, but they called after him and begged him to return to the raft. The Scientist dangled a key chain of interlocking rings made of sedimentary magnetite. Upon seeing it, Amir swam to the raft and climbed aboard. He was very thin. When asked how he had survived those many months in the sea, he replied that he had learned to catch fish in his mouth and to strain plankton through his moustache.

Even the Priest was glad to see Amir, having felt secretly guilty. He said a prayer, and then they collected enough food for a feast. Amir, wishing to contribute something, leaped overboard and soon returned with a Barkelonian flying trout clamped securely between his teeth.

More months passed, each day indistinguishable from the one before. At dawn the sun rose orangely from between the swells and settled in the evening into troughs that were different but looked the same. At night the moon and stars cartwheeled overhead, the constellations rotating in synchrony with the raft's position in the gyre.

After Amir's return they had shifted so that they occupied the points of a square. However, they were now too fat to move at all, even Amir. The Scientist caught fish and prepared the food, which he passed to the Priest. The Priest took his portion before passing the plate to the Engineer. After taking her share, she handed the plate to Amir, who returned it to the Scientist. The Engineer, who operated the stills, dispensed drinks in similar fashion.

For some time now the raft had been riding lower in the water, despite numerous patches applied by the Engineer. However, there were no patches left to apply. They noticed more dwarks circling than ever before. At night they could see piggy eyes glimmering just under the surface. The dwarks grunted loudly in the darkness. They heard it through the floor of the raft, a sound like sows rooting for truffles.

"I fear for us," said Amir, clutching his key chain, "but I believe in the sanctity of the stones."

The Priest squeezed his cross. Not to be outdone by a pagan, he said, "You should believe in God's Glory, my son, not in stones. It is He who looks after sailors cast adrift on life's turbulent seas."

"Well, hell," the Engineer replied, "if you have to believe in something then I believe in the strength of structures."

From his darkened corner the Scientist said, "I believe in the natural order of the universe and in nature's laws that hold it together."

They sat silently, each considering what the others had said. Amir was first to speak. "There is order in the stones," he said simply.

"And in God's works," answered the Priest.

"There is undeniable order in a blueprint," chimed the Engineer.

"And the order in nature is obvious to everyone," the Scientist said.

Suddenly they were unhappy, but at the moment darkness masked the dissatisfaction on their faces. Amir disliked the Priest's religious bigotry. He fantasized how his shipmate's fat carcass might burn for hours on a pyre, making him an excellent sacrifice to the stone gods on Zykrisikistan's sacred mountain.

In turn, the Priest could scarcely tolerate Amir's idolatry, in particular his tourmaline tooth and his prosthetic toenails of finely machined agate. Too bad, he thought, that putting heathens to the sword had fallen out of fashion. And the Scientist? God should banish him to Hades for such steadfast impenitence.

The Engineer looked at the Scientist's dim outline and loathed his smug, strigine face, his pomposity, the breadth of his knowledge. Her thoughts shifted to Amir. She became incensed upon remembering his description of houses in Zykrisikistan and how they consisted solely of doors and windows without roofs or walls. Did he think she was stupid?

The Priest was nearly invisible, but the Scientist could picture the old pederast's feet still encased in the rotten black socks he had refused to shed. They were naked now except for the Priest's socks and Amir's ridiculous swim cap. In his opinion the Engineer was undeniably clever at fashioning simple machines from materials at hand, but she was an ill-tempered, foul-mouthed cow who could provide a day's nourishment for an entire school of ravenous dwarks.

No one spoke the next morning, but instead looked at each other with anger and suspicion. At daybreak it was the Priest's duty to raise the sun screen over them, which he always did with exaggerated yanks on the lines. Afterward, he wound the lines securely about the cleats. But this morning he announced, "God knows, each morning I raise the sun screen over your sinful heads and lower it again at night, but does anyone ever thank me? Never! May His will be done. I quit." He pulled up his socks and made the sign of the cross. The sun screen remained folded.

Amir looked down at the air pump, which ordinarily he activated by pushing the plunger six times every hour. The work was not hard, but it required diligence. This morning he flung the pump aside in anger. "All day I pump air into our doomed craft, and to what purpose? So that unbelievers can live another day to blaspheme the stones! This tub can sink for all I care. The sacred stones on the ocean floor will embrace me in death; the rest of you are dwark nibblets." He glowered at them from under his swim cap.

The Engineer glanced at the two stills. It was her job to keep the modified fuel lines free of fouling algae and to fill the upper compartments with seaweed or seawater as the situation dictated. This morning she stated, "That's all she wrote, fellas. A man's home might be his castle, but I'm not a man and this ain't home. I'd advise you to go fuck yourselves, but you're too fat." She sat back and folded her arms. The stills went untended.

The scientist said, "Since everyone's being so goddamn selfish, see how it feels not to eat, because I refuse from this moment forward to fish and prepare food. We shall sit here in the sun looking at each other and oxidizing our own blubber. Just remember, the latest thinking in dwark biology seems to reinforce the fattest first hypothesis." He leaned back and looked at them condescendingly.

"What's the fattest first hypothesis?" asked the Engineer.

The scientist's voice assumed a professorial tone the others loathed. "Put simply, a school of hungry dwarks obeys a basic principle of nature's economy. To search for food takes energy. If the search is prolonged, extra energy is expended. To compensate, dwarks happening upon a school of prey seek out the fattest and most succulent individuals and eat them first because they provide the most nutrition per bite, so to speak. Then they eat the second fattest, then the third fattest, and so on. Obviously, the thinnest individuals might theoretically survive if the dwarks become satiated before getting around to them." He stopped talking and began to pick his teeth with a fish bone.

"I see," said the Priest after several minutes of silence had passed. He was watching the dwarks circling the raft and grunting through the gill vents on top of their heads. He turned sideways and untied the lines from the cleats and the sun screen went up. "I apologize for being selfish. Jesus loves the altruist."

Amir grabbed the pump and feverishly worked the plunger. The raft floated higher after his labors. "I too have been selfish," he said. "May the gall stones of my ancestors forgive me."

"A watched pot never boils," said the Engineer. With that she dipped a ladle of seawater and snatched up a handful of seaweed lurking in the trough of a swell.

"Anyone for breakfast?" asked the Scientist. He plucked mussels from the side of the raft and accepted similar gifts from shipmates. Amir, who seldom performed this feat before lunch, leaned his head over the side and strained a feast of krill, which he then recovered by combing his moustache over a pot of boiling water. Amir's immense buoyancy, combined with the ever-present dwarks, had ended his trout-fishing days.

The Scientist prepared a scrumptious breakfast of barnacles, krill, and bryozoans, and garnished it with sea lettuce. He passed the plate to the Priest, who threw up his hands in mock appreciation. "Oh, I couldn't possibly!" he cried. "I acknowledge the sin of refusing His bounty, but I have a touch of the gout, you know." The others knew he was lying through his priestly socks, but said nothing.

When the Engineer received the plate she turned to the Scientist and exclaimed, "Your feast is fit for a king, but I'm stuffed to the gills." The rest looked at her knowingly, but no one commented when she passed the plate to Amir.

"Ah, such beauty!" Amir was smiling at the plate and his tourmaline tooth caught sunlight reflected off the sea. "I could not disturb this plate for fear of spoiling its symmetry. Your presentation has the shape of a perfect crystal." So saying, he returned the plate to the Scientist. Amir's companions noted silently that the plate's contents had an amorphous shape more along the lines of a turd.

The Scientist received back the plate and made a show of examining it. "I felt some boils last night. Perhaps I have a mild anaphylaxis. If so, it would be wise to avoid mussels. And because everything is mixed together in a bouillabaisse, I ought to pass on this meal altogether." He set the plate aside knowing the others did not believe him.

In like manner, all inhabitants of the raft refused the Engineer's offer of wine at midday. Each had a reason, although none convinced the others of its truth. Lunch and supper were refused similarly, in each instance with a lame excuse. The next day was the same, and the day after, and the day after that. Because no one ate anything the Scientist stopped preparing food. Everyone refused wine, so the Engineer had no choice except to shut down the still. Their daily consumption became limited to a few sips of water.

As the weeks passed they grew thinner, and their belly skins hung as loosely as the pelts of hibernating bears. They drifted monotonously in the same southwest gyre under a sun that hung above them like a red ingot. Weeks became months. The raft rode ever lower despite Amir's pumping, and the dwarks circled closer.

During the day they sat under the sun screen and watched as swells dipped into troughs and emerged as swells again. Fat gawklets circled above their disinterested heads, and they barely noticed whole schools of Barkelonian flying trout hanging placidly in the raft's shadow practically begging for a hook.

They were exercising feverishly at night, each hoping to lose more weight than the others. With darkness the raft's interior became a maelstrom of movement. Its inhabitants grunted and sweated through set after set of sit-ups, jumping jacks, pushups, and leg lifts. They became lean and muscular, and their percentage of body fat dropped remarkably.

One day as they sat listlessly in the shape of a square, a dark smudge appeared on the horizon. The smudge grew larger with each passing hour, and by late afternoon had become a ship. For many months they had been flying the Priest's maniple. It fluttered even now, although its edges were tattered and its color had faded. The ship changed course and headed toward them, disappearing and then reappearing behind the swells. It was an oceanographic research vessel.

Abruptly there was a loud hissing sound as a patch gave way. The raft lurched and began taking on water. The castaways sprang to their feet and bailed frantically. Despite their effort the raft sank lower until bailers and dwarks were nearly at eye level. The dwarks gathered closer, grunting excitedly and bumping the raft from underneath.

The raft sank just as the rescue vessel arrived. Its four inhabitants, unable to reach the lifelines in time, were devoured by waiting dwarks. "We nearly got to them. A sad loss of life," the Chief Oceanographer remarked bitterly from his position on the bridge.

"Any loss of good data is even sadder," said the Assistant Chief Oceanographer.

His superior turned to her. "What do you mean?" he asked.

"This event was a perfect test of the fattest first hypothesis. Unfortunately we don't know which castaway was fattest, which was second fattest, and so on, nor can we verify the order in which they were eaten. If only I could have weighed them before the raft sank." She shook her head dejectedly.

"I see what you mean," replied the Chief Oceanographer. "The null hypothesis that degree of fatness is irrelevant still hasn't been falsified. Damn!" He slammed his fist into the instrument panel. "It's a crying shame!"

"A real pisser," agreed his assistant.

Internal Combustion
Explained

I was lying underneath a decaying Toyota saying something un-mentionable to its rusty muffler when a pair of spike heels click-ety-clacked over. White heels with bare legs sticking out. These legs rose out of sight at least above the rocker panels, maybe all the way past the door trim. They were upholstered in tan and looked smoother than calf-hide headrests.

I grabbed two handfuls of frame and pulled myself to daylight, thinking that no CAD program at GM could design knees like those. When I stood, the rest of the chassis came into focus. She had mahogany brown eyes, hair the color of two-oh-five radials, and the curves of a Jaguar XK8. She had little dimples on each side of a mouth that was candy-apple red and buffed to a high gloss.

She asked, "Are you, how you say, the mee*chan*ic?" The accent was heavy, but still lighter than a Ford LTD.

"That's me," I answered.

She narrowed those eyes and dragged them over my body like a damp chamois. After I was nice and dry, she said, "Well, mee*chan*ic, thees car, eet won' ron, you know?" She shifted a hip to one side and put weight on it. She twirled the key ring on her index finger.

I sauntered over to the car with her following clickety-clack and popped the hood. It was a Buick circa '83. I slipped the keys off her finger, jammed one into the ignition, and turned it. There was a grinding noise. "When you turn the key, an electric motor cranks the engine," I explained. "This makes the pistons move up and down inside the cylinders and causes the spark plugs to spark."

She looked at me without smiling. "These peestons, they move up an' down *slowly*, no?"

"Yes," I answered, "slowly at first, then faster and faster as things heat up. They're lubricated."

She licked her candy-apple lips. "Do they go, you know, yust up an' down or maybe a leettle from side to side?" To illustrate, she rotated her hips almost imperceptibly in a slow, rolling motion.

"Just up and down," I replied, trying hard to maintain professional composure.

"Hokay," she said. "Now tell me abou' theese sparks. Lots of sparkin' goin' on eenside, no? Where eet's lubricated?"

"Outside, not inside where the pistons are. When the pistons start going, air and gasoline get sucked into the cylinders after first having been mixed by a carburetor."

"I wanna know abou' theese sucking. I like to unnerstan' how my car, uh, how eet works." She crossed her arms, causing her breasts to spring up suddenly as if popped by a hidden clutch.

"Well," I said nervously, "The ignition ignites this air-gasoline mixture. The source is a spark from the spark plugs."

"Wery explosive, eh? I like that." She gave a little smile, never taking her eyes away from mine.

"Uh, yes. Anyway, the explosion is what forces the pistons down, powering the engine. Thousands of these tiny explosions keep the pistons in each cylinder moving up and down, up and down."

"You could say een an' out, een an' out, no? I mean, eet's the same, eh?"

"Sure," I said uncertainly. "You see, when a piston gets back to the top of the cylinder, another little explosion forces it down again. It's all happening very fast."

"Si, faster an' faster," she agreed. "An' all that sparkin' an' lubrication. It mus' be wery *juicy* eenside."

"Sometimes it can get a little too juicy," I croaked. "You can flood the cylinders. It happens if you pump her too hard while cranking the engine. All this gas comes spurting out prematurely and the spark can't get off."

"I know wha' you mean," she said, crinkling her nose. It was a perfect size for crinkling. "Sometimes wheen someone ees, how you say, cronking my eengine an' they flode too fast, you know? Theen my spark, she doan get off."

I was starting to sweat. "Yeah, I understand."

She eyed me appraisingly. "Why you cut you hair so short?"

"Uh, it's like my older brother's. You know, we like it short."

"Hokay, eef you say so. Now feex my car, no? An' wheen she feexed, come an' get me over there." She gestured toward the coffee shop across the street.

As she walked away all I could think of was Mario Andretti sliding into a turn at Indy and fishtailing out, taking that baby at almost two hundred per. She had those kind of moves. Then she stopped and turned around. "An' one more ting, hokay?" She looked me up and down again. "Eef you wash off that grease an' feex you nails, you maybe a good-lookin' señorita." She winked and added, "An' theen I show you wha' sparkin' ees reely like."

The Perennial Garden

SUNLIGHT WAS GLINTING PLEASANTLY off the razor wire when Birdie climbed onto the backrest of one of the institution's benches and tried to grip the edge with her toes. She teetered and waved her arms wildly before toppling backward onto the ground. "Damn," she said, sitting up and dusting herself off. "Can't seem to get my toes curled right."

Leonard, who was kneeling in the perennial garden, didn't answer. He never spoke unless there was something to say. He sat back on his heels and took a scruffy notebook from a pocket of his overalls and leafed through it, licking his fingers every few pages to make the process go smoother.

Birdie crawled over to him. She wasn't crippled like some of the others. Crawling just seemed more expedient than standing up and walking a few short steps before getting down again on hands and knees to be eye-to-eye. "Logically, it should work," Birdie said into Leonard's ear.

Leonard squinted past her at the horizon. "May 14th," he said decisively. Then he looked at Birdie and added, "I don't count crocuses or daffodils or tulips. I got no patience with anything that blooms amongst the snow. I told you before how I feel."

"But it ought to work," Birdie repeated. "Remember me explaining how birds can sleep on branches without falling off?" She then explained it again, knowing Leonard would have forgotten if he'd ever remembered at all. "When a bird bends its legs, its toes curl automatically. The muscles and tendons perform like levers." To demonstrate, she sat back on her own heels and bent one elbow, simultaneously curling her fingers. "Like this."

"May 14th," Leonard repeated, licking the end of a stubby pencil and slowly writing the date in his notebook. "Snow-in-summer." He gazed lovingly down at the silvery foliage and small white flowers just starting to appear. They reminded him of Mr. Battaglia with his silvery hair and pasty skin, before he had scratched out his own eyes. Poor Mr. Battaglia. Leonard's knees were resting just about on Mr. Battaglia's chest, give or take three feet of dirt.

"So a bird on a branch simply hunches down," Birdie continued, "and its toes lock in. Presto!"

Leonard consulted his notebook. "I'm thinking we'll see the first candytuft flowering on the 18th, if last year's date means anything."

"It really pisses me off." Birdie sounded agitated. She twisted sideways and sat up, the better to examine her feet.

Leonard looked at them too. "Watch where you step," he said. "There's tiger lilies coming up here."

"I think I see the problem," replied Birdie. "It's the sneakers."

"After candytuft it'll be spiderwort, Montana blue, Shasta daisies, wild phlox, catchfly, and the first bearded irises, in that order. Brings us right to the end of the month." Leonard closed his notebook and stood up.

"I'll be gone by then," Birdie said.

"You'll miss the Japanese irises on the first of June."

"They're letting me out." Birdie jumped suddenly to her feet and ran off across the lawn flapping her arms and honking.

Leonard wandered over to the catchfly and examined its ripening buds. The sticky stems would soon be shish kebabs of scarlet. He thought about Mr. Lowenstein who used to kneel on this very spot and bang his fuzzy head against the rocks. Leonard squinted hard, but the winter rains had washed away all traces of blood. Poor Mr. Lowenstein, now fertilizing the catchfly.

Leonard looked up and saw Dr. Mackiewicz's beret bobbling above the azaleas like a pram on a blossomed sea, guided forward by the short keel of the doctor himself. Dr. Mack negotiated the last bush, white Reeboks tacking smartly through a patch of withered daffodils, and approached Leonard. He seemed out of breath.

"There you are, Leonard," he huffed.

"Here I am," Leonard agreed.

"I want you drive Birdie downtown to the release site when Admin springs her, hmmm? She trusts you. Anybody else and we'd have to straightjacket her. Then she'd turn into a screamer and attract a crowd. We don't need any bad publicity here at Mental, not with cuts looming over us from State Budget." Dr. Mack pulled a notebook from an inside pocket of his fly-fishing vest. "Let . . . me . . . see," he muttered, flipping through the pages. "Yes indeedy, here it is. Looks to be the second of June."

Leonard consulted his own notebook and made a notation. "Columbine."

Dr. Mack tugged at his lederhosen. "What's that?"

"I said, columbine. Blooms the second of June. If last year serves as a guide."

"Columbine will do nicely," said Dr. Mack absently. "I'll see to the paperwork, hmmm? Are you taking your medication, Leonard?"

"Yessir, I was, except last year the poppies bloomed June 4th and the year before that it was June 13th, so I figure if God forgets to make the flowers bloom on schedule he won't pay attention to whether I take my medicine."

Dr. Mack stroked his beard and stared into the distance through glazed eyes. "I see, yes, of course, that's splendid. Keep up the good work, Leonard. Now . . . when is our next private consultation?"

Leonard checked his notebook. "Could be either blue sage or yarrow, if last year's any guide."

"Fine, fine. Well, it's been fun, Leonard, hmmm? Keep up the good work. Glad you're taking your medication. A good doctor always stays in touch with his Guests, am I right?" He beamed up at Leonard. "See you at Group this afternoon."

"Yessir," Leonard said, shouldering his hoe.

At Group, it was Birdie who got things rolling. "That's Gertrude and Helmut out there," she said, pointing to the window. On the ledge were two pigeons. "They're expecting."

"Oh my," said Dr. Mack. "Isn't that wonderful, people? Isn't that terribly wonderful?" Several heads nodded, and Ms. Bates beat her nonparalyzed arm spastically against the side of her wheelchair and drooled onto the floor.

"They've just laid a clutch of eggs," Birdie continued. "It takes seventeen to nineteen days for pigeon eggs to hatch."

"Well now, we've all learned something important, haven't we?" Dr. Mack was tugging nervously on his lederhosen. "Does anyone have a comment, hmmm? Leonard?"

Leonard was already paging through his notebook. "Fleabane," he replied. "June 14th, if you can believe last year."

"I wanna talk about shipses," said Mr. Kupidlowski.

"Yes, of course," agreed Dr. Mack. "Let's turn to the subject of ships. . .""Not them kinds of shipses," Mr. Kupidlowski interrupted. "*Shipses*."

"Woof! Woof!" Ms. Swanson, her eyes bugging out like a frog's, had begun to bark.

"I've got it! I've got it!" Mr. Morrison leaped out of his chair. To him, everything was a game of Charade. "It's barque, isn't it? A barque is a kind of sailing ship. You see, it was Ms. Swanson's clue. So I'm right, aren't I? I win, don't I?"

"Not shipses, *shipses*!" Mr. Kupidlowski repeated. "Ba ba black shipses. Those is the shipses I mean. You shaves them and makes cotton."

"Yes, of course," chimed in Dr. Mack. "Now, we all know why Mr. Kupidlowski is a Guest here at Mental, don't we? Does anyone remember, hmmm?"

"Bestiality," piped Birdie. "He buggered an ostrich when he worked at the Zoo. Poor thing had gotten its head stuck in the fence." Birdie bent over and grabbed her ankles and wiggled her rear end in Mr. Kupidlowski's face. It was true that the elegant ladies who strolled the city's avenues were safe from Mr. Kupidlowski, but the same could not be said of their yorkies and miniature schnauzers.

Birdie had returned to the window and was cooing softly at the pigeons. She turned to face the room. "The parents feed the babies by regurgitating pigeon milk from their crops. I've been practicing for when I have squabs of my own." She rolled her stomach in and out several times and upchucked expertly.

"Truly outstanding, Birdie," said Dr. Mack, lifting his Reeboks just in time. He tugged furiously at his beard. "Yes, a splendid example of nature's many adaptations. Can anyone add anything, hmmm?"

Ms. Bates beat enthusiastically on the side of her wheelchair. "Woof! Woof!" barked Ms. Swanson, dropping to all fours and sniffing one of Dr. Mack's chair legs.

"I wanna watch *Lassie*," said Mr. Kupidlowski.

"Not until after Group," Dr. Mack replied.

"Then I wanna talk about shipses. I love shipses, especially the little white fluffy shipses."

"He means the lambs," Birdie explained.

"Their little ears is so soft," said Mr. Kupidlowski.

"The lamb's ear," Leonard interjected, "bloomed June 27th. Of course, that was last year."

"Yes, Leonard, which brings us to you. Can anyone tell Dr. Mack why Leonard is a Guest here at Mental, hmmm? I'll give you a clue. Serial."

Mr. Morrison leaped to his feet. "Bowl!" he shouted. He frowned and rubbed his jaw, then thrust his index finger at the ceiling. "No, no, wait! I have it now. Yes, now I remember. He's a crazy serial kill-er, that's why!" He sat down and rubbed his bald head and tugged on his skinny nose. "Do I win again? Do I?" He looked at his shoes and started to cry softly.

"That's correct, Mr. Morrison," Dr. Mack said brightly. "Yes in-deedy, you win. My, but you're good at this game." Mr. Morrison looked up and smiled sadly. "And Leonard is getting better, aren't you Leonard?"

"Yessir."

"You see, people? Leonard always takes his medication. Let that be a lesson to everyone. Leonard is even allowed outside sometimes. Isn't that wonderful progress?" Dr. Mack beamed at everyone in turn.

"When Leonard first came to us he couldn't associate his victims—actual human beings—with those despicable acts of violence," Dr. Mack continued. "But that's no longer true. Now then, Leonard, describe to us here in Group some recent associations you've been able to make, hmmm?"

Leonard opened his notebook. "May 14th. Snow-in-summer. Mr. Battaglia. May 27th. Catchfly. Mr. Lowenstein. . ."

"We don't quite understand, Leonard," Dr. Mack interrupted. "Could you perhaps explain in more detail?"

"Yessir. Killed 'em with my hoe. Buried Mr. Battaglia under the snow-in-summer because of his white hair. Planted Mr. Lowenstein in the catchfly." He looked up from his notes. "Mr. Lowenstein's hair was red."

"But Leonard, both men were let loose at the release site in town with Admin's approval. You drove them there, hmmm?"

"Yessir, I did. Then killed 'em with my hoe. A real hard tap on the back of the neck set 'em down for good."

"Woof! Woof!" said Ms. Swanson, who was sitting on her haunches and panting.

Leonard glanced at her. "Dogwood. May 15th by my reckoning. Last year, anyway."

"I could have got that one!" shouted Mr. Morrison. "It isn't fair. Leonard used a notebook."

Dr. Mack crossed his stubby legs and farted delicately. "We're simply stunned by Leonard's remarkable progress, aren't we people? Isn't it wonderful? Remember that the capacity to form abstract associations is one of the very definitions of consciousness. You're to be congratulated, Leonard."

"Yessir. Does Admin want me to do Birdie two weeks from now?"

"An interesting question, Leonard. Admin works in mysterious ways, hmmm? Okay, let's end Group by giving Leonard a round of applause. He's our hero for today!" Group ended on a loud note of banging, barking, and clapping.

Time flew with all the weeding. Not a moment could be spared Leonard to murder anyone, much less dig a hole for burial. If it wasn't sheep sorrel it was cat's paw, dandelion, clover, or goosefoot. Russian olive sprang up everywhere, and lurking underneath the mulch were the pale stems of bittersweet with their red roots, and multiflora roses flaunting embryonic spines.

Three weeks had passed since Birdie's release, and she was presently impersonating a pigeon in Town Square. Leonard had visited her once before when he drove in to buy slug bait. On this day he found a shady parking place for the pickup and strolled across the square, noting with dissatisfaction that the beds of impatiens needed weeding.

"Hi, Leonard," Birdie cooed. She was on hands and knees cadging handouts from people sitting on the park benches. Leonard sat down on one himself.

"Hi, Birdie. I brought you some popcorn."

"Just sprinkle it on the ground."

He emptied a portion of the bag at his feet and watched while Birdie scrambled with the other pigeons to gobble it up. Finally she stood and licked her lips, which were covered with sand. "Hey thanks, that tasted good. I've been practicing flying," she announced. "Remember me telling you how birds can fly? It's because of their enormously developed pectoral muscles and their bones, which are hollow and extra light." She stuck out her chest. "I've been working on building up the old pectorals. What I need now is altitude." She flapped her arms up and down ineffectually. "I figure to glide from this bench to that one over there by July 15th "

Leonard opened his notebook. "Gayfeather. That's the closest I can come to the 15th. It flowered July 10th last year, but might be later now, considering the cold spring."

"I should be seeing a little progress by the end of this month."

"Let's check," Leonard offered. "I got hosta and blue hydrangea on the 30th and Thomas Killian daisies on the 27th, taking into account last year."

"Are you going to gut me, Leonard? Cut out my gizzard and pluck my feathers and bury me in the perennial garden?" Birdie climbed onto the bench beside him and started to preen herself.

"I got to associate you first, like Dr. Mack says."

Being a pigeon impersonator, Birdie tried not to look too thoughtful. "I guess there's pigeonberry."

"Never heard of it," Leonard replied. "I got no use for daffodils either. Anyhow, Ms. Bates is next. James parks her wheelchair wherever I'm working so she can watch. Yesterday she drooled all over the orange Maltese cross just as it was coming out. James says Admin is springing her."

"Springing Ms. Bates?"

"Sure. Now that budget cuts have come up, Admin figures she can survive on her own, especially with the circus in town. Well, look, I got to go water in this slug bait. Worst year I've ever seen for slugs. They ate hell out of the delphiniums."

Weeds became less troublesome as summer progressed, and Leonard eventually found the time to do Ms. Bates with his hoe. Admin's instructions had been to drive her into town and dump her at the release site, but to return with the wheelchair. It was listed on Inventory. Admin filled out the paperwork, faxing copies to all parties on the usual distribution list. Under Anticipated Survival Methods, Dr. Mack had written that Ms. Bates could probably slide along on a trail of drool in the manner of a garden slug, propelled by her one good arm. Leonard buried her underneath the Maltese cross. The entire patch had suffered an attack by gypsy moth caterpillars—not to mention having been slimed repeatedly by Ms. Bates—and was doing poorly anyway.

At next Group, Dr. Mack was twitching with excitement. "People," he announced, "I can't believe our good fortune. State Budget has given Mental its highest Release/Return Ratio Rating." He beamed at everyone before continuing. "We've had no returns from our releases for two straight years, which translates, by State Budget's calculations, to an Assumed Cure of one hundred percent!" He hiked up his lederhosen and sat down. Ms. Swanson barked while everyone else clapped.

"And naturally, Assumed Cure legally becomes Actual Cure after two years, provided said releasee has not been returned here and Board approves his or her Cure by a two-thirds majority. State Budget has assured Admin that it's practically in the bag. We're on the verge of a perfect score, people, meaning no budget cuts for us here at Mental during the next Fiscal. Isn't that simply fantastic-wonderful, hmmm?"

Dr. Mack opened a file folder in his lap. "I've just returned from Records and thought you'd like to remember some of those fortunate Guests who have undergone therapy here at Mental and been released into successful lives. One of the more recent, of course, is Birdie, who's paying her own way in society as a pigeon impersonator. Does everyone remember Prof. Macintyre, the esteemed lepidopterist? His recurrent nightmares during which he pupated and writhed around on the floor, hmmm? Leonard?"

"Yessir, got 'im right here." He removed a grass blade from between his teeth and paged through his notebook. "July 21st, by last year's calendar. Try underneath the butterfly bush."

"What a splendid association!" Dr. Mack exclaimed. "How about another." He made a buzzing noise.

"I've got it!" Mr. Morrison became suddenly animated. "The movie *The Fly*. Flies are insects, too. I'm right, aren't I? Don't I win?"

"Not this time, Mr. Morrison," said Dr. Mack sympathetically. Mr. Morrison looked at his shoe tops and started to weep. Dr. Mack continued, "I'll give you a clue, people. Our deranged apiculturist. Went around stinging Staff and Guests alike with her hat pin. Defecated in jelly jars and tried to convince everyone it was royal jelly. Somebody? Anybody recall her name, hmmm?"

Leonard tapped his notebook. "Says right here, July 6th. Mrs. Grodin. Fertilizing the bee baum as we speak."

"Your associations are truly astonishing!" replied Dr. Mack.

"It spreads pretty thick over two years, bee baum," Leonard noted. "Doubt if she could be dug up right off. But we'd get her eventually. Wouldn't do the garden much harm either. Bee baum transplants real easy. If we had to dig her up, of course."

"Of course!" chimed in Dr. Mack. "Well, people, what do you think? Are there any others who've left here for success out in the wide, wide world? Let's put on our thinking caps, hmmm? Mr. Kupidlowski, you could help us here. Think hard. You remember Mrs. . . . . ah, come now, Mr. Kupidlowski!"

Mr. Kupidlowski furrowed his substantial brow. "I love the little shipses so much."

"Mary!" yelled Mr. Morrison. "It's got to be Mrs. Mary, because she had a little lamb with snow-white fleece. You can't keep me from winning this time!" he crowed.

Dr. Mack ignored him. He also ignored Ms. Swanson, who had just urinated at his feet. He glanced at the yellow stain now wicking up one of his Reeboks.

"But this Guest had a white poodle," Dr. Mack said. "Now do you remember?"

"Yes, yes!" exclaimed Mr. Kupidlowski. "It was like a beautiful little shipses. A little white shipses. I want to work on a farm for shipses and shave them to make cotton. I want to be a shipses shaver."

"And its owner, remember her, hmmm? That was Mrs. Martin." Dr. Mack looked sternly at Mr. Kupidlowski. "We were treating her nymphomania and you nearly ruined everything by sneaking into her room and buggering the dog. That incident lowered her self-esteem immensely, Mr. Kupidlowski." Dr. Mack clucked his tongue disapprovingly. Mr. Kupidlowski looked suitably ashamed.

Leonard said, "The poodle's pushing up dogbane in that field near Admin. Mrs. Martin's under the pussy willow patch by the woods. They're weeds, the both of 'em, so there's no dates. I got no patience for weeds or for crocuses either."

"I think I see, Leonard," mused Dr. Mack. He stood and tugged fiercely on the ends of his moustaches, ignoring the lederhosen crinkling around his knees. He bent over absently and patted Ms. Swanson, who licked his hand gratefully. "Yes, well, let's end Group by giving Mr. Morrison a big hand. You got most of them, Mr. Morrison, and you're our hero for today." Dr. Mack said it with a smile, but his mind seemed elsewhere.

In mid-summer Dr. Mack filled out paperwork committing himself as a Guest. Admin did not replace him, preferring to improve the bottom line by saving a salary. In late August, State Budget rewarded Admin for its perfect Release/Return Ratio Rating by transferring its employees to the capital and giving them jobs in Financial Planning. This was partly because the Speaker of the House owed the Director of State Budget a favor. The head of Admin at Mental, it turned out, was the Director of State Budget's brother-in-law, and his Admin Assistant, with whom he was having an affair, threatened to blow the whole deal unless he took Staff along and guaranteed everyone raises.

"Nobody's running the place," Leonard said to Birdie. They were sitting together on a park bench in Town Square. Birdie had cocked her head and was watching Leonard intently, trying to make her eyes look beady.

"Coo," she replied, sticking her nose in her armpit as if preening feathers on the underside of a wing.

Leonard took out his notebook. "Dr. Mack checked in when the Turk's cap lilies flowered. That was August 2nd. This year, of course. By northern hibiscus time they were hauling away the desks and file cabinets." Birdie cooed again, ending on a higher note. "When was that? Let's see. August 17th. Then Staff said they needed two weeks of vacation, which took us through Labor Day weekend."

"Goddammit," Birdie said, speaking for the first time. "Here I am, biological clock ticking, and another squabbing season down the drain. You want me to go back with you, Leonard? I'm not having any luck around here as a pigeon. See that two-timing piebald male up there?" She jerked her chin toward a window ledge on the third floor of City Hall.

When Leonard didn't answer, Birdie continued, "Took up with a little blue-barred chippy, slim and trim. God, I cried for days. No more preening each other, no more dumping on statues together. But that's it. Cheat on me once, I'm gone. Vanished." She made a sweeping motion with one arm.

"It's time for the mums and Japanese anemones." Leonard squinted past her. "Then there's the voles to deal with, and white-footed mice eating my bulbs." He clasped his hands in his lap.

"I'm thinking of becoming a duck," Birdie announced. "Never

could perch worth a damn, not with these feet. As a duck I'd just have to stand around wearing flippers and crapping on the lawn. Quacking is a helluva lot easier than cooing." She gave a loud quack, startling the pigeons waiting expectantly for a handout. "Take that, you bastards."

"Dr. Mack says us Guests at Mental can run the place ourself and take turns leading Group, no problem. There won't be any releases now that Admin's moved out, but I got plenty of mulching to do, and there's fall fertilizing. And they gave me a new job walking Ms. Swanson. Dr. Mack's been trying to housebreak her, but he's only got as far as newspapers."

"I'm going with you," Birdie said, hopping off the bench. "You ever considered duckhood?"

"Duckweed?" Leonard asked. "I don't count duckweed. Got no patience for tulips either."

Baked Scrod

It LOOKED LIKE ANOTHER restaurant, nothing special, a set of double doors in a strip mall. At the entrance, set within a weatherproof glass case, was posted the menu with the heading Bill of Fare. On it were the prices of meals with four dollars subtracted from the regular price for Early Birds, people who got there and ordered dinner before six-thirty. The time was five o'clock on a Sunday.

Every other business in the mall was closed, and the lot was mostly empty. He parked near the entrance to the restaurant and stepped out of his car into sunlight the color and temperature of day-old tea. The Bartlett pears planted in open recesses around the parking lot had begun to flower, although he was not one to notice such things. Flowers were what women noticed, not men. He associated flowers with dreaming, and women were dreamers. A man had more important things on his mind. Practical things.

He opened the door and went in. Straight ahead were wooden tables and chairs of some commercial make in Early American style. Early American for the Early Birds, he thought. To his left was a counter that held a cash register and a stack of menus. A man of forty or so—younger than he was, certainly—came out from behind the counter. "Hello, would you like a table?" the man asked. He was wearing a maroon pullover; he had short brown hair that hung straight down around the circumference of his head.

"Sure, Mark," he replied amiably. He was, after all, a salesman, and friendliness was a tool of the trade. He took pride in noticing little things, such as a person's name tag.

Mark picked up a menu and led him into another room. It was decorated like the first. Mark put the menu down on the table of a booth and left. The man slid into the booth, noticing that the back was straight and uncomfortable. He should have requested a table, but most had been set up to accommodate four or more people. At least Denise is here, he told himself. He could suffer through any discomfort knowing Denise would be his waitress.

He looked down at the paper place mat. It said Welcome to the Hearth 'N Home and listed five other locations in addition to Falmouth. They were Plymouth, Centerville, Yarmouth, Hyannis, and Orleans. All of them no doubt nice, he thought, but only Falmouth could boast of Denise.

She came toward him grinning, carrying a glass of water. She was slightly built with large breasts. Hi," she said as if out of breath. "Glad you could make it for Early Bird."

"Wouldn't have missed Early Bird or seeing you," he answered, not taking his eyes away from her chest. "I was hoping you'd be the special tonight." He looked up at Denise and laughed, and she laughed with him. It was an old joke, a tired joke. Every salesman in America had said the same line to a waitress at some time, but Denise—God bless her—laughed anyway. A tribute to Denise or her youth? He couldn't be certain.

"It's really hot in here," she said, and blew at a dark curl that had escaped from underneath her cap. All the waitresses wore Early American costumes: white ruffled caps and aprons and long gray dresses that hid their legs. But he could see Denise's legs. In his mind he reconstructed their shapes from the slender ankles turned inward and the shuffling, fetching walk. A brief glance was sufficient. His personality at once relaxed, expanded, becoming comfortable upon assembling for itself a whole woman from a dustbin of mostly invisible parts. He was, he told himself, the patient archaeologist of his own imagination, capable of reconstituting feature by feature the female physiognomy from a few tantalizing clues. Nothing was ever lost or misfiled; the tolerances, the discerning eye, were exacting. In a salesman's life the freeways are too long, the time between clients too extended, for error to accumulate or imagination to be shelved.

He rested his elbows on the table and built a steeple of his fingers, and when that was finished he rested his chin on buttresses of joined thumbs. Long ago a woman had complimented him on this mannerism, remarking that it made him look sophisticated and cerebral. He had never forgotten. "They ought to turn down the heat," he said sympathetically. If Denise noticed the placement of his chin, she made no sign.

"We told Mark already, but Mark says get used to it. Mark says there'll be lots of seniors here because it's Mother's Day, and seniors get cold.." Her New England accent rendered every r to ah, and Mark became Mahk. It was cute. Irritating, but cute. He would get used to it, just as she would adjust to his Midwestern accent. Denise's youth was an advantage. The young adjust faster. After their marriage, she would be first to settle down and accept routine.

"I'll get your rolls," she said. As she walked away he noticed how the uniform made her hips look wider. This is poor salesmanship, he thought, and made a mental note to bring it up with Mark.

Denise returned with a basket of rolls, and he glanced once again at her ankles. He fantasized about grasping one in each hand like a drumstick and sliding forward to kiss her bare navel. For an instant decorum's opaqueness vanished, and he became excited thinking of her lying before him naked and vulnerable. She seemed helpless, trusting.

"Here's the preliminaries," Denise announced, setting down the basket. "Dressing on the salad?" She straightened up and took out a note pad, unconsciously pushing back the dark curl with her free hand.

What an endearing trait, he thought. So young, so awkward and coltish. "What do you recommend, sweetheart?" He smiled up at her pleasantly.

"Well, me personally, I like the raspberry vinaigrette, but that's just me. Ranch is popular too, especially with the older crowd."

"Why don't we let them have it, then?" he replied. "The older crowd, I mean." He laughed and reached for a roll.

"Sure," she said with a giggle. "We're gonna sell a few gallons of it tonight, that's for sure." She rolled her eyes, and they both laughed again, co-conspirators. "Ready to order?"

"Not just yet. I like a glass of wine before dinner to settle the stomach, prepare for the ordeal ahead. Digestion is a form of war, you know," and he raised the roll and shook it like a weapon between them. "It's the digestive juices against the food, both armies in there battling sword against shield. Better to send an ambassador first, if you know what I mean." He winked and put the roll back in the basket.

"Sure," she answered. "Wines are listed on that little card." She reached over and extracted the list from between the salt and pepper shakers. As she pulled back, her breast brushed his arm.

The little fox! he thought. Teasing me. Old fashioned I'm not, but still, we agreed to save it for the wedding night. I told her, save it and the honeymoon will be something special. Let's have it be special, and she agreed. But she's making it tough, the little vixen. Maybe I won't wait for the wedding night. Maybe I'll take her right on the front seat of the car before driving her home. Just lift up that Early American dress and demonstrate what's in store.

Denise straightened up, seemingly unaware of her act. She brushed back the curl again. "Boy, this heat! Well, we've got some specials that aren't on the menu. Want to hear them?"

"Love to," he said. He stretched one arm across the back of the booth. The gesture announced confidence, masculinity, and possession of the space around him. Space that included her. Let her now be pulled into the center of his power. It was all so easy, like throwing popcorn in front of a pigeon.

She pulled a handwritten list from the pocket of her apron and read from it. "I'm supposed to start out saying, 'Chef Georgio offers these additions to his menu tonight,' but I can't do it." She giggled and let the hand holding the list drop to her side. Then she said in a low voice, "His name is just George, and he's not, like, from Italy or anything. We went to high school together."

The man laughed softly, a laugh no louder than her giggle. He whispered behind his hand, "The secret's safe with me."

Denise grinned. "Well," she said professionally, "we have roast turkey with stuffing and giblet gravy. We have baked ham with honey-mustard sauce. And finally, there's scrod baked in white wine and lemon butter finished with seasoned bread crumbs and served with baked beans. Standard New England cooking, this last. They all come with a choice of potato or rice and veggie of the day, except for the scrod. That comes with a veggie but no potato or rice. Whew! That's a lot to read."

"Bring a glass of the house cabernet, please, Denise. When you bring the salad, that is. Meanwhile I'll look over the other choices and be ready when you get back." He spoke the words firmly as if addressing a subordinate, and having said them looked down at the menu. Don't be too friendly, he told himself. Young women admire a certain aloofness in a man. It's time she understands who makes the decisions.

"Okay," Denise replied, and moved off.

The restaurant was filling up, and she did not return immediately. When she did it was apologetically. "We're out of cabernet. Sorry. I brought you merlot instead. Mark says it's the closest thing to what you ordered." She took the glass of wine and the salad off the tray and set them in front of him.

"I'm certain this will be fine." He looked up at her and smiled. It was a moment for magnanimity, for letting her know all was forgiven and that she could now take pleasure in serving him. She smiled back, guilelessly, he thought, and he began to doubt her sincerity.

Denise took the pad from her apron pocket. "Ready to order? I'd get mine in soon if I were you, unless you want to stick around an extra hour." As if in explanation, she glanced over her shoulder at the room, which was filling up rapidly.

"Right," he replied almost brusquely. "Now enlighten me. A 'scrod' is . . . what?" He was starting to perspire. The room was definitely overheated.

Denise tried to blow the curl away from her eyes, sympathetically, it seemed, but it remained stuck to her forehead. He watched this gesture with interest. Here was a woman who knew humility, who went out of her way to save, not her own image, but his! Quite remarkable for one so young. She was saying to the world, this is my man, *my* man. He never sweats, at least not unless the whole world is sweating too.

There was a pause while she looked at the wall beyond his head and seemed to grapple with an inner conflict. "Well," she answered finally, "some say it's a baby cod, and some say it's fish left in the hold of a dragger that are too squashed to identify." She met his eyes and grinned. Then, having come to a decision, she leaned down and cupped a hand to his ear. He was aware of her breast pressing lightly against his shoulder. "And some," she whispered, "say that 'scrod' is just the pluperfect of 'screwed,' that it doesn't mean anything."

He jerked his head back, electrified. Quickly collecting his wits he exclaimed in mock embarrassment, "My goodness!"

He was suddenly fatigued, as if overcome by an indeterminate malaise originating from the oppressive realities of age and gravity. His hand, which had been resting unobtrusively on his thigh, crept to his stomach, and what the hand felt was tautness in the shape of a melon. Youth had hurled itself at him like a burning torch, and his visceral response had been to jump aside. When Denise threw back her head and laughed, he laughed too, pretending to be nonplussed, afraid she had noticed his unease.

"Then the choice is made, sugar." He spread his arms as if conceding the final point of a contest in which she was the winner. "Scrod it is." With a flourish he closed the menu. "And I'm ordering another glass of this delicious merlot in advance." His acting had been pointless. Denise wrote down the order without a word and strode off to wait on a nearby table.

As she moved away, nostalgia washed over him unexpectedly like a rush of feverish surf, and his eyes filled with tears. These bouts of weeping occurred now with increasing frequency and apparent randomness. They arrived on surprising emotional winds, their passing leaving a hollow space, and into this unnerving void, creeping like shadows, came feelings of inadequacy, fear, and indefinable shame.

He looked blindly at the tables peopled by gray heads, everything dissolving now in rivulets as if seen through a rain-streaked window. An old man came into his line of sight with slow, shuffling steps, the cane's rubber tip touching soundlessly against the floor. Had this man's life also been wasted, his dreams unfulfilled?

He looked down at his clasped hands and marveled at their hairless bulk and papery texture. The shiny skin, reflective even in this dim light, was a sure buzzard attractant, mortality's messenger. He opened one palm and examined the lifeline. It was short and intricate and unpromising, not that such things mattered any longer. Had he ever really lived? He recalled those few moments of excitement when he had risen higher than other men, drifted into the clouds enveloped and suspended in euphoria, and they appeared like reluctant apparitions. It occurred to him that not even memory had been kind, looping out of sight without a visible beginning, forecasting even in these bright flashes a lingering despair and a grudging sorrow.

There was a paper napkin, and he used it to wipe his eyes and then his forehead. After draining the rest of the wine, he looked around for Denise. When she glanced his way he raised his glass discreetly, and she nodded. Every table was filled. Without his noticing at first, the noise level had escalated, becoming a subdued buzz reminiscent of a beehive in an otherwise silent room. The idea of insect sounds masquerading as speech was not too farfetched, he told himself, but this thought was quickly discarded as irrelevant, even unmasculine. He was not a proponent of abstract reasoning. No, he told himself, he was a practical man, not a dreamer, a man needing a glass of wine.

Denise strode to his table with such energy that he felt the turbulence of her movement. "Can you believe it?" She was grinning. "It's just crazy. I mean, look at all these people!" She set down the glass crookedly, causing some wine to spill. "Sorry about that," she chirped, and was gone.

He wiped the bottom of the glass with his napkin and took a sip. I like her energy, he told himself. Yes, that kind of enthusiasm can make a man feel young again, inspire him to lose weight, acquire some energy himself. There were many good years ahead for the two of them. He would drop some pounds, probably twenty-five or thirty, get down to fighting weight. Watch the old cholesterol, cut out unnecessary calories like cream and sugar in coffee, switch to a low-fat diet, give up desserts. With the prospect of a young wife, necessary sacrifices were on the horizon. But worth it in the end. Why not start now? Why not, indeed? He felt better already. Morose behavior was stupid, especially for a man of determination and confidence. Willpower. All that life required of the successful was willpower, and he had it in spades. He raised his glass in a silent toast.

He was finishing the salad when Denise arrived with his entree. "I hate to tell you," she said as if bringing bad news, "but there's a line outside the front door all the way to the parking lot. All seniors."

He leaned back in a signal for her to pick up the salad plate. "You'd think all mothers were senior citizens," he replied with a smile.

Denise laughed. "Here's your dinner. Enjoy." She set the plate before him and was gone.

He broke all four rolls in half, buttered the sections, and set them in a ring around his plate. The food was decent, but not memorable. His fish was dry on top, the baked beans pasty and sweet as if poured from a can, the summer squash soggy. The portions, however, proved exceptional, and by the time he had eaten everything he was no longer hungry.

The ambient low-frequency noises of the room were punctuated now by women's laughter, and he heard the clink of ice in glasses, of flatware on china. Chairs scuffed softly against carpet or banged woodenly against tables. Mark's brown head bobbed intermittently above the gray sea. Previous feelings returned, diffusing into remote corners of his consciousness like the molecules of a colorless gas until he recognized nothing and no sound was familiar.

"Care for dessert?" Denise was bending over him collecting his dishes. She set one edge of the tray on his table to steady it. "You okay?"

"I'm fine. Guess the heat's getting to me."

"Yeah," she replied, "it's a regular oven. At least the front door's open now, with the line of people." She blew ineffectually at the curl.

"What do you have?" he asked.

"We've got apple and cherry pie, chocolate cake, chocolate and vanilla ice cream, and strawberry cheesecake. I'd go with the cheesecake, but I have to warn you, the stuff has about a million calories."

"Cheesecake looks great on you," he said with a smile. "You're nice and slim. Guess I'll have the cheesecake with two scoops of vanilla ice cream on the side." Then he added, "Anyway, I'm starting a diet tomorrow."

Denise ignored both the compliment and notice of his impending diet, concentrating instead on steadying the tray with her hip so that her hands were free. "Got it," she said, and wrote the order on her pad. "Coffee?"

"Sure. Cream and sugar. One cup will do, no refills necessary."

"Coming up." She stuffed the pad into her apron pocket, hoisted the tray, and disappeared into the crowd.

Denise returned promptly with his dessert and coffee. He ate slowly, savoring each bite, finally spooning up the small puddle of melted ice cream. Denise, who was watching all her tables, took notice when he had finished and brought the bill.

"How was everything?"

"Excellent," he replied. "And you were right about the cheesecake. I'm in big trouble now." He patted his stomach and tried to look rueful.

"Well," Denise said, "here's the damages. Stop by if you're ever this way again."

"I sure will," he replied, hoping to conceal the falseness in his smile. Yes, there are years ahead, he told himself. Good years yet to be lived, but not with Denise, definitely not with a flirt like her. He could certainly do better. He left the correct amount of money on the table, including a fifteen percent tip. The service had been good but not extraordinary. Not worth twenty percent, the amount he planned to record the expense account. He looked at his watch. Time to phone home. A married man with three grown kids ought to call his wife on Mother's Day.

The Anniversary Call

I TELEPHONED MY PARENTS to wish them a happy anniversary. Sixty years is a long time to be alive, much less stay married to the same person. I placed the call when I figured they were finished with supper and had the dishes cleared away. They never go out to eat any other time, so it stood to reason an anniversary would be just a typical day, sixty years or not.

The phone rang three or four times before someone picked up and said hello. It was Mom. Dad never answers the phone, not even if Mom is out shopping or visiting Aunt Marge or playing bingo down at the Senior Center. I once asked him why, but he didn't answer. Dad's policy has always been to not answer stupid questions, and I guess this one qualified. Once in school a teacher told us, the class, there's no such thing as a stupid question, but when I relayed this information to Dad, know what he said? He said that any question from a kid is stupid. So there you have it. I was about ten, I guess, when I stopped asking Dad anything. It didn't seem to make him happier.

"So how's it feel?" I asked Mom, trying hard to inject a little gaiety into my voice.

"So how's what feel, my arthur-itis? It still hurts like hell. You expected by some miracle it went away?"

"No, silly, I mean sixty years. How does sixty years feel?" There was silence. I could hear Dad doing wheelies on the kitchen linoleum. Something metallic fell with a clatter.

"Hold on," Mom said, "I dropped a spoon." She set the phone down on the counter with a clunk, and I pictured her bending over painfully and picking up the spoon from off the floor. After a while she came back on the line.

"How come *you* didn't get that spoon, you're closer than me."

"I'm in Iowa, Mom, remember? And you're in Buffalo."

"Not you, dummy. *Him.* How come you didn't get that spoon? You were closer to it than me." Then I realized she was talking to Dad but speaking into the mouthpiece like it's Dad who lives in Council Bluffs.

Dad said something I couldn't hear. "What did he say?" I asked.

"What did who say?"

"Dad. What did Dad just say?"

"I don't remember. What did you say?" She was still talking into the mouthpiece, although I knew the question had been directed at Dad. I heard Dad's voice in the background then Mom said, "He can't remember, but he wants to tell you himself."

I heard another receiver being lifted off its hook, and suddenly we were in a three-way conversation. "Hi, Josie," Dad said. "I went in the living room and got the other phone. It's one of those, uh, what kind of phone is this, Mother?"

"It's a cordless phone," Mom replied. As an afterthought she added, "It's one of those phones without a phone cord."

"It's a cordless phone," Dad said.

"Gee, that's great!" I exclaimed, reaching with effort for a little excitement. "All the modern stuff, huh? And by the way, this is James, not Josie."

"Hah!" Dad snorted into his receiver. "We got a remote control for the TV, too. I bet you poor bastards out there in New Jersey don't have remotes."

"Iowa," I corrected. "And it's James calling."

"He lives in *Iowa*," Mom admonished. "How many goddamn times do I need to say it? *Iowa!* Don't you know your son from your daughter?"

Dad ignored the outburst. "I'm a little deaf," he answered by way of explanation, "and all the nagging in the world won't cure deafness."

"So now I'm a nag?" Mom asked. "So after all the care you get, I'm a *nag?*"

"The care?" Dad replied. "You call this *care?* I'd get better care down at the funeral home. I'd get better care at Frank Perdue's chicken farm. Hold on, I'm coming back to the kitchen. These wheels don't work so good on carpet." There was a pause followed by a whirring noise.

"Well," I continued, "how does sixty years feel?"

"What sixty years?" Dad asked. "It's not my birthday. Is it your birthday, Mother?"

"No. My birthday's in August, or don't you remember? You probably don't remember, but I'm used to it."

"Today is Saturday," Dad said firmly. "I'm looking at the calendar now, Josie. It says Saturday, plain as day."

"It's James," I said. "And today's your sixtieth wedding anniversary. So how do you feel?"

"I feel terrible," Dad replied. "How would you like to live in a wheelchair? They come get me Wednesdays in the special van and take me downtown to the Center so I can play bingo with the other old farts."

"That's great!" I exclaimed. "It's important to keep up your social life, right Mom?"

"You play bingo on Thursdays," Mom said, "not Wednesdays."

"Social life?" Dad asked incredulously. "More like social *death.* Nobody can remember anyone's name from one week to the next. It's introductions all over again, everybody's new. 'Hi, I'm Ralph,' says some dipshit across the bingo table. And you reply very carefully, so you don't sound senile, 'Say, Ralph, haven't we met before? I'm sure we've met before, probably last Wednesday.' And the guy sitting next to you chewing a big smelly cigar that it's against the law to light, he says, 'You're senile. This is Ralph's first visit, but I'm here every Tuesday. What's your name again?' Some social life."

"I'd feel a helluva lot better if my knees didn't hurt all the time," Mom said. "Just try doing housework with my knees, and cooking, and shopping for groceries. Walk a mile on *my* knees. Tell me the last time you dried a dish or mopped a floor." She was talking to Dad, of course.

"What's your problem?" Dad answered. "I can't even feel my knees. Anyway, who mops floors from a wheelchair?" Dad started to cry and hearing him was unnerving. I was unprepared for role reversal in which he became the child and I the adult. The sobs were gentle and brief, ending as abruptly as they began.

Mom waited until he finished before yelling into the receiver, "You! You're my problem! And now you're a crybaby on top of everything else!"

I held the phone away from my ear so the buzzing in my head would stop. I was thinking, there they are in the same room, not five feet away from each other, and what happens? I call to wish them Happy Anniversary and they get into an fight courtesy of AT&T.

"Hey," said Dad in his argumentative tone, "it wasn't me that went apple picking out in Oregon and got laid by a farmer."

"Jesus Christ, I was *nineteen*. That was 1933, and you and I hadn't even met. Anyway, it was Washington. I was never in Oregon."

"It was '34, and you should have known better. You might have had a little consideration for me instead of thinking only of yourself."

"It was '33. I remember what year I was nineteen."

"There's a word for what you are. It's *slut*. You are a selfish little *slut!* You call this care? Being wheeled around by a slut, having a slut cook your food, handle your knife and fork?"

Mom started to weep. "I never should have told you," she blubbered. "Ever since the day we got married, I can't remember how many years, you've thrown that in my face."

"Sixty years," I interjected.

"Don't interrupt your mother when she's berating someone," Dad admonished. "You're not so big I can't take a belt to you."

Mom had stopped crying and was merely huffing. The sound was loud and moist and reminded me of when I was little and a calf at the Erie County Fair snuffled in my ear. "You're a real shit, do you know that?"

"Who, me?" I answered, instinctively defensive.

"Who's there?" Dad asked.

"It's James," I replied.

"James. Well, why didn't you say so? You've upset Mother, and I'm going to strap you good when you get home."

"I'm calling long distance," I said. "I'm not coming home."

"Long distance?" Dad seemed confused. "Then hang up now. You can't afford it."

"I'm a lawyer," I said irritably, "and I can afford it."

"He's a lawyer, Father," Mom repeated. "He can afford it."

"Horseshit," Dad said. "He's a paperboy. He can't be making more than two bits an hour. No wonder he doesn't have one of these, uh, what kind of phone is this, Mother?"

"It's a cordless phone. A phone without a phone cord."

"Right. Well, James, you better go. You can't afford this call. And don't come around begging us for money when the phone company shuts off your service. I never figured you'd amount to a pinch of shit, and I was right. I doubt if you even own a remote for your TV."

There were two clicks, then a dial tone. "Happy anniversary," I said.

Cesspool of
Contradictions

IT WAS A VILLAGE FROM which no one escaped, and those who did were sensible enough to never return. Civilization had long since gathered up its belongings and moved away leaving behind only superstition and the uncertainty of memory. The citizens of this village—old, young, and some who were neither—lived squeezed between the sea's edge on one side and dense rainforest on all the others. But where an ocean vista might have brought comfort and coolness there remained only tangled mangroves and buzzing mosquitoes that swarmed in thick clouds offering the illusion of a breeze.

History, as much as history can record about such a place, gives its name as El Beso de la Luna, but a moon's kiss seemed incompatible with the odor of wallowing tapirs, of outhouses and rotting vegetables and dog shit moldering on the paths. Maybe, someone suggested, the name had actually been El Beso de la Luna Canonizada, raising the question of whether the moon was ever sainted, even the Spanish moon of long ago in the age of saints.

One day, out of curiosity and nothing else, a delegation went to the rectory and asked if there had ever been a woman named Santa Luna.

Father Dudando, whose name means doubtful, was dozing in the afternoon heat. He rolled over in his hammock. "No, said the padre," brushing flies from his face, "I never heard of a Santa Luna, but you can never be sure when God's works are concerned. As for this village, whatever its name, God can't misplace what he has never found. Now that you've interrupted my siesta please find the angelic one and ask her to fix me a plate of beans and fish. And tell her to wear the red dress when she brings it." He meant Angélica, of course, the village whore.

There the situation remained, going neither forward nor backward, until an idler named Eusebio, a teller of lies and one who cheated at dominoes, suggested solving the problem simply by renaming the village El Pozo Negro de Contradicciones, which means cesspool of contradictions. And so it came to be called.

The new name might have been its own contradiction were the contradictions it embodied not contradictory. Instead of a traditional village with houses, a church, and a market, El Pozo Negro de Contradicciones consisted of a banyan tree. It was a plant of immense proportions, having been growing outward from that place since the time of Methuselah, or so said Father Dudando.

According to Old Vivo the tree had once marched out of the forest and directly into the sea as far as the horizon, but the length of years had caused it to shrink, just as he himself had shrunk. Some discounted Old Vivo's story because his memory had become like a net of holes without string in which nothing is retained, including the fish. Not that it mattered. The massive tree had spread in so many directions that the original trunk was now lost in a labyrinth of prop roots descended from the sky to become trunks themselves, and by the lattices of aerial roots dangling and swaying like lace curtains across windows of perpetual twilight.

There was not another tree like it, certainly none emitting this feeling of dryness and certainty. Even during the wet season no raindrops penetrated its dense umbrella of leaves. The branches and canopy offered such snugness and security that the villagers had established permanent domiciles in their shadows, walled away in the privacy of mossy façades. Some had lived for generations in these spaces, willing them to their progeny who willed them to their own progeny, and so on.

Ancient paths through this forest within a forest eventually became thoroughfares marked by names and arrows carved into the trunks. Children shrieked and cavorted through the maze, dodging chickens, dogs, and herds of snuffling pigs that softened the earth with their rooting, earth that would otherwise have been packed hard by human feet. Passing monkeys dropped turds on unwary residents and pelted them with rotten fruit, abetted in this general frenzy by loose-boweled toucans and parrots. Had it been a contradiction El Pozo Negro de Contradicciones could just as easily have been named El Pueblo de Sombreros.

The village barber arrived at a certain buttress of the banyan tree every morning except Sunday. He set a cracked mirror in a crotch of low limbs, draped a towel over his shoulder, and hung up a worn strop. He set the bucket of water at his feet and took from a satchel his gap-toothed comb, an ancient shaving brush made of a boar's bristles, a razor, and a dish of soap and laid them in a row along a branch shaped conveniently like a shelf. After unfolding the chair he placed his apron over the back of it, an apron his wife had made from a worn sheet. Those who wished to sit comfortably while waiting brought their own chairs, and for the rest there was the ground.

The barber was known as El Seco, which means the dry, because he sweated profusely both day and night. The first thing he did upon opening shop was to shave himself, mindful always of the barber's paradox. The fault was Eusebio's, a name that means pious.

What a joke, thought the barber. Eusebio who read books that had bobbed up to his very door on a day long ago when he should have been fishing. It was Eusebio who had sat thoughtfully in the folding chair one morning and asked through the lather, "If the village barber shaves everyone who does not shave himself, who shaves the barber?"

Old Vivo, whose name means spry, unfolded himself painfully from the ground. "That's easy," he said. "The barber shaves himself every morning before he shaves us. He's been doing it for years. He finished up just before you sat in his chair."

"Yes," Eusebio had said, "but the barber shaves only those who don't shave themselves, so if he shaves himself then he doesn't."

Faustino, whose face was veiled that morning by a hanging root, was the next to speak. "The answer is obvious," he said, "provided the barber doesn't shave himself."

To which Eusebio replied, "The barber shaves everyone who does not shave himself, so if he doesn't shave himself then he shaves himself, an impossible situation. Either he does or he doesn't."

"Either he does or he doesn't what?" asked Pensativo, whose name means thoughtful.

"Ah," said Esmeralda, the village beauty who sold trinkets from a rickety table just around the next prop root. All conversation stopped abruptly as each man silently interpreted that voice as for him alone. Esmeralda cleared her throat. "Obviously," she said, "the barber is a woman."

"Not so fast," said Eusebio. "If the barber is a woman, either she shaves herself and is one of the people not shaved by the barber, or she doesn't shave herself and is among those shaved by the barber."

"But women don't shave," said Pensativo.

"And your name should properly have been Pánfilo, which means simpleton," replied Eusebio.

After Eusebio had wiped the soap from his face and gone to loaf by the sea the rest said unkind things about him, including Esmeralda, whose beauty had failed to inoculate her mouth against gossip.

One aspect of El Pozo Negro de Contradicciones that could not be called contradictory was the passage of time. Had it gone by quickly that would have been different, but instead it crept so slowly that each day seemed to persist a week, a week lasted a month, and so on until nobody thought about the days at all, including the holy days, which even the padre forgot. Every day, in fact, passed at the speed of the one before, and tomorrow was destined to pass no sooner or later than today. Time, the villagers remarked to one another, rushes by on the back of a crippled snail.

The church was located deep inside the banyan near its embryonic beginning where the air was unmoving and nearly black, perhaps similar to the first air of the world. In that tenebrous place the people could no longer imagine clouds, making any thoughts of heaven impossible. It was alive with worms and eyeless snakes, of buttresses and hanging roots dripping with fungus and the slime of toads. The holy water had evaporated years before, and owls now nested in the basin. Nothing human moved or spoke. In such a silence prayers can sound like admonitions.

Father Dudando no longer held mass and had stopped hearing confessions, telling everyone he saw in the course of the day to say a few Hail Marys and ask forgiveness for whatever sins they had committed, not forgetting imaginary ones. Children grew up unbaptized, the dead were buried without rites, and couples lived openly together out of wedlock. People celebrated festivals having no religious purpose, often dancing and drinking far into the night when the flapping robe of the good padre could be glimpsed among them.

And what should have turned scandalous did not. Of the women only Angélica the whore had blue eyes. Several of her dozen or so illegitimate children were blue-eyed too, and although Father Dudando was the only male villager with blue eyes no one had yet put two and two together. News of Mendelian genetics, like everything else, was still a good distance away from El Pozo Negro de Contradicciones.

Needless to say that events of today closely resembled those of yesterday, and the prospect of tomorrow being no different was as predictable as the sunrise. Consider that if the scenery never changes, neither do the objects inside it. Until one special day when everything changed. Which day of the week was it, and what month? No one can say.

Eusebio awoke late that morning as usual and pulled on his trousers. He sat up in bed and placed his feet squarely on the dirt floor, which was not far below where he sat because the mattress was on the floor too. He yawned and scratched for a time before standing. Celestina, whose name means heavenly, was making coffee on the other side of the buttress, so he followed the odor.

Celestina glanced up. "You slept in again," she said. "You're lazy.

Even a pig works harder at gathering fruit pits dropped by the monkeys. How long has it been since you fished? A week? A month?"

Because terms relating to time were without meaning in El Pozo Negro de Contradicciones, Eusebio had no trouble answering: "I don't remember, but probably longer than a day. Anyway, in this hot weather the fish don't bite, and even if they did I have no bait because the mudflats are too dry to dig. Then there's the boat. . ."

"Yes, the boat," said Celestina. "Let's not forget the boat, that water-soaked pile of rotting wood sinking from the weight of barnacles. Drag it up here. I'll set it afire and cook your breakfast over the flames."

"I'll look at the boat and check its condition," Eusebio said.

"Do that," said Celestina, "and while you're there chop away some of the mangroves to let in a breeze. Here, take your machete."

She held out the tool, but Eusebio ignored her. He took a cup of coffee and trudged the short distance down a path into the mangroves where his boat was tied. Their home, located between the two outmost buttresses of the banyan tree, faced the mangroves and beyond them the sea. A realtor in El Pozo Negro de Contradicciones, had there been one, might have described the location as cozy with an ocean view, the only vista being a thick wall of mangroves.

Eusebio came to the end of the path where his boat listed to one side. Through the clear water he could see barnacles attached to the hull, one atop the other, feathery feet moving rhythmically in and out of their shells. Around them floated an extended forest of filamentous algae. The air was hot and thick with the moisture of possibilities. Nothing seemed alive except barnacle feet and schools of pilchards darting among the mangrove roots.

A sudden splash cleaved the silence as if a large fish, or perhaps a dolphin, had leaped out of the water and landed on its side. Eusebio peered cautiously around, seeing only the effect of the sound as ripples reached his boat, making it bob leadenly and tug weakly at its bow rope. He stood for a time in that spot sipping coffee and slapping absently at mosquitoes until boredom and hunger turned him toward home.

Celestina handed him a plate of beans and bread straight from the coals. Eusebio sat on a stump and started to eat. "I heard a large fish jump by the boat," he said.

"With luck it'll jump into the boat and we can eat it," Celestina said. "That's the only way you'll catch it. Here comes your worthless friend Faustino, so I suppose I'll have to feed him too." She went to get another plate.

Faustino, whose name means lucky, sat down carefully on a vacant stump. Faustino was albino and could not venture into the light without sunglasses. These being a rare commodity in El Pozo Negro de Contradicciones, Faustino's had been repaired many times until only one lens remained. The other opening had long ago been covered with a piece of wood cleverly carved by Eusebio.

It had been Faustino who sat hidden behind the dangling root of the banyan that morning when Eusebio brought up the barber's paradox, and to use the term hidden is no exaggeration. In addition to albinism Faustino had suffered since childhood from a mysterious disease that turned his skin into a substance resembling the bark of a tree that has eaten too much sulfur. These warty growths eventually covered his extremities until his arms and hands resembled branches. His legs became two trunks with flattened bottoms, and he walked with a slow shuffle, as an uprooted tree might walk if miraculously granted this ability.

Celestina returned with a plate of food and a spoon and began to feed Faustino. "You're shedding again," she said, noting with a nod the bits of darkened skin that always collected around him like crispy sawdust. "I wonder," she said, "do you have nightmares about carpenter ants?" With this she laughed so hard that she was forced to set down the plate for fear of spilling its contents.

"I'm sorry, Faustino," she said finally, wiping her eyes. "Next I'll be spoon-feeding my husband whose hands have become nearly as useless from doing no work. Look at them. A man's hands ought to be calloused, but Eusebio has the hands of a librarian, which is no wonder because all he does is read his books and cheat at dominoes. And drink."

As the men were finishing breakfast two others showed up, not to eat but to play dominoes at Eusebio's table by the edge of the mangroves. El Seco, sweating as usual, carried his barber's chair. Father Dudando carried nothing but a musty respect of holy office, and Celestina quickly relinquished her own folding chair for him.

"Why aren't you cutting hair?" asked Eusebio.

"Because it's Sunday," El Seco said.

"Then why isn't our fine priest saying mass?" It was Eusebio again.

"Because today is Monday," the padre said. "Anyway, we came to play dominoes with you and the Tree." They gathered around the table, shifting to make room for one another. Father Dudando had meant Faustino, of course, who by now was accustomed to the nickname El Arbol.

"You're shedding," El Seco said to Faustino across the boneyard, as piles of dominoes are called.

"Maybe you should shave him," said Eusebio. Everyone in the village knew Eusebio as Faustino's protector, and sometimes this responsibility required him to speak in Faustino's place.

"Shave what?" said El Seco. "You can't shave bark. His face is like the bole of a kapok tree with two eyes looking out."

"If El Pozo Negro de Contradicciones had a sawmill we might plane him, said Father Dudando," which sent Celestina, who was sweeping the floor inside, into peals of laughter.

Eusebio looked directly at the padre. "I'd expect more humanity from you."

"God works in mysterious ways, Eusebio," replied the padre. "If He chooses to turn people into trees who's to say it isn't part of some heavenly scheme?" He sighed and looked at Faustino. "Think of Job's trials," he said, "and be comforted."

Faustino tried to scowl, but the muscles of his forehead were stuck fast. Even narrowing his eyes had become impossible. "I feel like a man in a tree's body," he said in return. And he added, "I don't know if a tree can feel like shit, but I do."

That afternoon after his friends had gone home for siesta Eusebio sat on his stump whittling a stick. It was a stick consisting of several diverging branches giving some the appearance of legs and another of a head. But a head of what?

Unknown to Eusebio Paquito had crept up behind him. Paquito shouted "*Boo!*" in Eusebio's ear, causing him to jump and nearly cut off Paquito's nose with his knife.

"Dammit don't do that," he told Paquito, who by now was sitting on the stump opposite him.

"I'm sorry, Abuelo, but I think of you as one of my friends, not as my grandfather."

"A grandfather with a heart ruptured by fear," Eusebio said. "Now what does this look like?" He held the stick against the sky.

"A stick? A whittled stick?"

"Use some imagination. I see a dragon. Look again. Here's the head, here's the tail, and these are the legs."

"It's either a dragon dragging one leg behind it," said Paquito, "or a three-legged dragon. One or the other."

"I see what you mean," Eusebio said, "but here's the thing. My book of P" (by which he meant volume P of his encyclopedias) "says that in philosophy an object or image can't truly resemble something imaginary. One picture of a unicorn is as accurate as another because unicorns don't exist, and a carving of a dragon with three legs and a tail is as good as a dragon with three legs dragging a fourth behind. So my dragon doesn't have to be one or the other. It can be both or neither, although whichever you chose would be irrelevant, understand?"

"No. But I don't care. I have ten years, and in two more I'll be grown. Then I can leave for the city and ride a motorbike and never come back to El Pozo Negro de Contradicciones."

"Not even to see your old abuelo?"

"No. I'm not coming back."

Just as Eusebio was about to reply when suddenly loud splashing sounds came to them through the mangroves, sounds like a boat capsizing. It was accompanied by groans and bellowing such as a drowning bull might make, or a bull who has just tasted the pain of a matador's acero.

Eusebio and his grandson hurried down the path and on arriving where the boat was tied they saw something that perhaps no other human beings had seen before.

———————

What they found was a scaly creature with a darkened back and lighter belly thrashing around in the shallow water, evidently trapped by the falling tide. Unable to reach the channel it was flailing about and groaning pitifully, as some fishes do when taken out of the sea. But this fish, if indeed it was a fish, appeared to be larger and more rotund than any citizen of the village except possibly El Flaco the village butcher, whose name means the skinny.

Details were hard to discern in the late afternoon light, which bounced off the water and around the mangrove roots, and the water thrown up had touched their eyes and made them sting. Paquito stood quivering behind his grandfather, gripping the ragged legs of that good man's trousers, peering out now and then to get a brief glimpse before turning away and wiping the salt from his face.

Finally, after the creature quieted down, the two observers could see a row of fins down its back, what could be two short arms and two equally short legs all ending in fins, and a hideous face with bulging eyes and thick lips and hardly any nose.

From behind them Eusebio and Paquito heard Celestina shouting, "What's that noise? What's going on down there? Eusebio, answer me or you'll regret it the rest of your life."

"I've already regretted it my whole life up to now," Eusebio muttered to Paquito, who simply stood there open-mouthed. "What is it, Abuelo? Is it a fish?"

"No," Eusebio said. "Perhaps a reptile. We must go back and check my books." They returned up the path where Celestina waited.

"What's happening?" she asked.

"It's a dragon, Albula," Paquito said. "A huge dragon with gigantic teeth."

Celestina turned to Eusebio. "Is this true?"

"We didn't see any teeth," he said. "And we can't be sure what it is until I check my books."

"Always your books," said Celestina. "Eusebio the librarian. Why do you think the answer will be in your books? You were once a fisherman and should know about the sea."

"Not now," said Eusebio, and reached for volume R. He lit a candle and turned to the section on reptiles, but could find no mention of large sea-dwelling kinds except crocodiles. There was one lizard bearing a certain similarity that fed on seaweed in the cold seas far away. However, it had a long tail and appeared to be smaller than the creature they had seen. And that was all. He flipped over the last page and sighed with disappointment. The incomplete knowledge had left a vacant space inside his head, causing what he did know to tilt one way then another, like a ship's gimbal. He paged through the section on reptiles again, showing Paquito the pictures.

"It's not any of these," Paquito said when they finished, "so it must be a dragon."

"I agree," said Eusebio, thinking of the stick he was whittling and also that he should consult volume P and again read the part about reality and representation. Could it be that his books were wrong?

Paquito ran off to announce that a dragon now lived among them. Eusebio returned his book to its proper place and blew out the candle. "Do you want to see the dragon?" he asked Celestina.

She flapped a hand in front of her face as if warding off a bad scent. "No," she said. "I'll see it when I have to."

Eusebio strolled down the path toward the water, stopping once to uncover a bottle of aguardiente hidden among some leaves. By the time he reached the water his boat had diminished to a silhouette. He held the bottle to the sky where just enough light remained to illuminate the single swallow that sloshed back and forth like a tiny captive ocean.

The dragon was still there, fat and exhausted. It lay on its back, the silver scales of its large belly showing dully. Eusebio squatted down and touched its arm. The creature flinched and shifted slowly toward him, lifting its head until its eyes came into view, large and luminous. The mouth opened as of if to speak, emitting nothing but a series of rapid croaks such as certain fishes make when pulled from the water on hook and line.

Eusebio unscrewed the cap and emptied the contents of the bottle into the creature's mouth, causing it to swallow reflexively. There followed a bout of coughing and more thrashing at least as violent as before. Eventually both activities subsided, and the dragon lay there blinking. Now the darkness was nearly complete. Eusebio waded the few steps to his boat, where he lifted up a piece of loose decking and returned with a full bottle of aguardiente. In passing he stooped and patted the dragon's head, hoping to reassure it as he might a nervous dog.

The dragon flinched at his touch and ducked its head underwater, but soon he could once again hear it breathing. Eusebio opened the new bottle and took a long swallow, then reached for the dragon's head and felt around for its mouth. The lips were hard and slippery as a fish's. With a steady hand he poured a healthy jolt between them. This time there was no coughing but instead a satisfied smacking sound.

In the distance he heard Celestina calling. She said, "Eusebio, has the dragon eaten you? I hope for your sake it has because the pain of being swallowed is nothing like you're about to feel if you don't come home right now."

"The problem with living on the land," Eusebio said to the dragon, "has mostly to do with suffering. If you have ears then you know what I mean." He took a pull on the bottle and dispensed another to his prone and water-soaked companion. He then told the dragon several things, including the paradox of the village barber. He asked the dragon if it might be Catholic, in which case a priest was available to hear confession and dispense the Eucharist, provided the padre was up to such tasks, naturally.

He was asking the dragon about its early dragonhood when he suddenly became dizzy and toppled over. Above the buzz of mosquitoes he heard crude music coming off the water. It drifted gently toward him on the nonexistent breeze, sounding like a lullaby of croaks and gurgles rising swiftly through tinkling bubbles of the thinnest glass. If the corals could sing, he thought before passing out, how sweet their music would be.

And that's how this day in El Pozo Negro de Contradicciones, a day that began like all the others, eventually ended.

———————

Eusebio awoke to a sensation of his body rocking, thinking he might have fallen asleep in the boat, but the reverie was interrupted by a sharp pain. Upon opening his eyes he saw that he was lying on the ground and Celestina was kicking him in the ribs.

"Wake up, you drunken pig. When you didn't come home I pictured in my mind a night of debauchery with Angélica, but I should have known that your love of aguardiente is greater."

Celestina stopped kicking him and sat down to rub her foot. "Look at you, curled up and hugging that bottle of moonshine like a beautiful woman. An empty woman, considering you and your bloated friend consumed her every drop."

Eusebio rolled over and saw the dragon, still lying on its back in the shallows and snoring loudly. "I've been traveling," he announced with his head still resting on earth. "You accuse me of drunkenness when what lies here is an exhausted man needing sleep. You thought I was awake all night drinking with *that*?"

"I've seen you pass out while lecturing El Arbol's dog, the black and white one that pisses on its master's leg thinking it's a tree."

"That dog is very intelligent," Eusebio said, "and where someone pisses has nothing to do with anything. Old Vivo often pisses on his own leg."

"I admit, Eusebio, your lies are always interesting. So where did these travels take you if not to Angélica's house? Obviously you didn't go by boat because yours is still rotting in the mud."

"My mind and body traveled through air," Eusebio said.

"Ah, then you dreamed this lie you're about to tell me."

"No, it was real, although a certain few—and I include myself—possess a hidden organ no civilized medicine could ever find. Its function is to dream. But there I was, so high that mountains looked like anthills. I floated, little more than a feather, down through pink clouds among squadrons of curious dragonflies, twisting ever so slowly, until I landed on a beach of loud surf where at evening the horizon rolled like an eyelid over the orb of the sun. People ran out of their huts to greet me thinking I must be a god. It was strange because they could hear only with one ear, the ear opposite the sound, and they had no eyes. It took some adjustment on my part, let me tell you, certainly beyond the abilities of an ordinary man in so short a time. They begged me through their mouthless faces to stay and rule them, but I declined. The experience was harrowing, and I barely made it back to you, Celestina. Thank God we're together again."

Eusebio sat up and spread his arms. "You know," he said, "that the ground is just the floor of a room and for a ceiling we have blue sky. Here we live, trapped inside invisible walls. If you look around the monkeys know this, and so do the parrots, even ants and lobsters. And what do they know? That nothing matters except making love and procreation. So come join me, Celestina, the ferns can be our mattress."

"You were always the poet," Celestina said, "but right now I can't decide which of you is more disgusting," meaning him or the dragon. She stood and strode up the path bumping into others who had come to see the creature described to them by Paquito.

Eusebio stood too. He smoothed his trousers and tossed the empty aguardiente bottle into the mangroves. "Ah, my friends," he said, as the first villagers appeared. "You've come to see El Dragón, but I regret that he's still sleeping. Life has been hard for him in such shallow water. We must get him back to the depths."

The villagers gathered at the end of the path, the taller looking over the heads of those in front, the shorter hoping to get a glimpse between the legs and underneath the arms of others. Small children were hoisted onto their fathers' shoulders for a better view, and soon each person, from nursing babies to crones and geezers, had been jostled, shoved, wedged, or lifted into position to observe.

"This is a very fat dragon," someone said, and there were murmurs of agreement.

"Does it swim on its back?" asked Old Vivo.

"It must, and that gray thing is its sail," said Pensativo.

"That's the stomach," Eusebio said.

"I wonder if it's edible," said El Flaco, visually measuring the possibilities for chops and steaks, loins and bacon.

Angélica bent down for a closer look. "I can tell it's a manly dragon," she said.

"The important thing is whether he's Christian." Having spoken, Father Dudando pushed to the front. "We can't have pagans living among us." The truth of this remark might have puzzled an outsider stumbling upon a whole village gone pagan, more or less, including the padre, but in El Pozo Negro de Contradicciones it was merely contradictory.

The commotion had awoken the dragon, and he lay where he was blinking in the unfamiliar light. He groaned as if in pain and attempted to address his forehead with a cool wet fin, but his arm was too short.

"It's a hungry dragon," someone said.

"He's a sea dragon," Eusebio said, "so he probably eats fish and seaweed. But that doesn't matter because we should push him out to sea to swim away. Come help me."

Several men waded into the water and along with Eusebio began pushing the dragon out of the shallows among the mangroves and into the channel that led directly out to sea. In fact, you could see low breakers in the distance falling over the bar. It was only a short way from where they stood to deeper water.

"This is like pushing a loaded barge," El Seco said. "I've never felt anything so heavy. Even El Flaco would seem weightless." He stood huffing and sweating and rubbed his sore back. El Flaco pushed as best he could, although his immense stomach kept him from bending over completely, and he could only push a little with his arms extended. Old Vivo, resembling a wet scarecrow, was no use whatever. And El Arbol could do little except remain planted on the shore, nearly invisible among the trees.

Most of the men stayed on land, afraid the dragon might bite them. In the end it was Eusebio, Father Dudando, Pensativo, and Paquito who did the work, rocking the dragon back and forth as you rock a skiff stuck on a mudflat and eventually breaking him free of the mud's grip. Then they waded along pushing him toward deeper water as you would a log. A final shove and the creature was adrift on the outgoing tide. And that was the last of the dragon, or so they thought.

When he noticed himself floating away the dragon started to bellow and moan, reminding everyone of a calf newly deserted by its mother. Even Celestina's heart nearly burst—Celestina, who had walked away and then crept back behind the crowd—and she pleaded with Eusebio to go fetch him. It was Paquito, the best swimmer in the village, who actually rescued the poor creature, shoving him near enough so that everyone capable of lending a hand could help ease him into the shallows beside Eusebio's boat. For his part the dragon seemed relieved and gave out what the villagers took to be contented sighs.

"He's slippery as a fish," Paquito said to Eusebio. "And he has no handles so I had to push him instead of pulling as you would a person. Now what can we do?"

"We take him home," Eusebio said simply.

———————

Easier said than done, and maybe impossible had it not been for a contradiction. In the opening sentence of this story it was stated that no one who left the village ever returned, the exceptions being those who did. One of these was Modesto, whose name means moderate and sober. Before leaving to discover his place in the world Modesto had been the village drunk, but having reached the city he went into rehab, underwent job training upon getting out, and became a traveling salesman of straw and turnips.

Fate was kind that morning because who should show up at Eusebio's door hoping for a game of dominoes but Modesto riding on the seat of his donkey cart. He heard the noise at the end of the path through the mangroves and walked down to learn the cause. What he found was a village greatly in need.

How is it that people observing the same event can each bear separate witness? A hapless dragon in the eyes of the villagers was to Modesto a potential customer for his entire load of mattress stuffing, if not the turnips. When asked to help he naturally complied.

There ensued more activity than El Pozo Negro de Contradicciones was likely to experience in an entire year, however long that might be. Dozens of machetes chopped down the mangroves, widening the path so Modesto's cart could be driven to the water's edge and backed around, after which dozens of hands pulled and lifted, voices grunted and swore, until eventually the dragon lay atop the straw and turnips. Celestina was gratified to suddenly see water instead of mangroves from her front room, although she later complained how Eusebio's derelict boat ruined the view.

They unloaded the dragon beside Eusebio's outdoor table among the stumps. He seemed exhausted, or at the least hung over. Released from the shadows his every feature now stood out, and it was apparent that El Dragón was very old, in dragon years probably surpassing even Old Vivo, who had ridden with him atop the cart and of whom he seemed especially fond.

Father Dudando went to the church and returned with some holy water that he sprinkled on El Dragón, which caused him to twitch.

"Will that help?" Pensativo asked.

"Help what?" said Father Dudando.

"Help make him Catholic," Pensativo said.

"I doubt it," the padre replied, "but it ought to be good for his complexion. His skin seems to be drying out."

"It can't hurt," Eusebio agreed. "If you're related to a fish even holy water is better than none at all."

What does time matter? Shiny novelty corrodes eventually to sameness. Hours lie trapped under the pressure of days waiting to be released one by one. Like birds suddenly free of their own shadows they flap away never looking back. Angélica became pregnant again, acquiring a waddle and a belly that peeped out of her tunic with increasing boldness, but this was scarcely news. The children, as always, followed her like chicks expecting her shuffling steps to expose a treat from the leaf litter. Modesto fell off the wagon, more accurately his donkey cart, without spilling a drop of aguardiente from the open bottle that was now his constant companion. Practiced skills are easily reclaimed. It was Old Vivo who discovered Modesto whimpering in the mud and instead of calling for help sat down with him to share a drink.

Angélica's unborn child could be Modesto's, or so claimed Esmeralda. The womb is not windowless, and maybe this unseen fetus gazed accusingly through its mother's navel where the skin is thinnest, an eye pressed against that bright spot. Modesto's visits did, in fact, seem timed to the length of gestation, no more, no less, and when he waved goodbye and drove off in his cart Angélica held a purse filled with copper coins. The experience was a zero-sum game if Modesto had left behind another hungry mouth's worth of debt. Poverty can be chewed, but after swallowing the taste remaining is only emptiness.

Eusebio remained untouched by these and other occurrences because he possessed two remarkable gifts. The first was an ability to disappear into his own presence, no small achievement in a place where nothing passed without comment. According to the padre, in the unlikely event of a government census Celestina would undoubtedly be recorded as widowed. Eusebio, according to El Seco, is a man who can be bearded one day and clean shaven the next and no one would notice the difference. And El Flaco? "I put my thumb on the scale when weighing Eusebio's chicken," he admitted, "and he still somehow cheats me. I think I'm watching him, but my thumb becomes lighter and the scale always tips in his favor. All my life I've dealt with weights and measures, but this can't be explained."

Eusebio's second gift was a capacity to be satiated under the weight of abstinence. This was most apparent following poor sugarcane harvests when the village distillery had to be shut down temporarily. Sugarcane is a weed and grows rapidly, but not fast enough in drought years to suit a thirsty village. In fact, such times led to considerable hardship, forcing cancellation of festivals and parties and slowing the hands of the clock even more. Then the few who had made their own aguardiente from forest fruits and shown the perspicacity to store it became much admired and even modestly wealthy, at least until the next cane harvest.

Eusebio was never at anyone's mercy. He stayed drunk through good times and bad, always with a supply of aguardiente on hand. And yet no one ever saw him perspire over a hot still or solicit drinks from friends. Even Celestina was mystified. He told her that his endless store was a benefit of good planning, strategies learned from his encyclopedias, especially the volume containing a section on inventories and how to manage them through lean economic cycles. Had anyone examined his boat the real reason would have become clear at once: although just a simple sloop of six meters, the ample space beneath its deck was crammed with liter bottles of aguardiente. Barnacles had not induced the list, but a shifting of the cargo over months and years as Eusebio extracted bottles one at a time.

—————

No story has just one ending because life's events—and even life itself—are conditional. Just a small change in their sequence reverberates through the system affecting everything in unpredictable ways. This story is no different. Blame Angélica who missed an appointment to entertain El Seco while trying to remove a spot from her red dress, or Celestina for burning two crooked pieces of wood at the same time. Maybe the fault lies with Old Vivo's last tooth, lost while biting down on a cigar, or Father Dudando, who impaled his hand on a dorsal spine while patting El Dragón on the back, or perhaps El Flaco who ran short of chicken parts at his shop and substituted his neighbor's best hen. No one can say with certainty if any of these occurrences affected the ultimate outcome.

Then there was Eusebio's boat, which he never once took to sea. He found it abandoned one day, bobbing among the mangroves at the end of his path, the hold stuffed with bottles of aguardiente and a complete set of encyclopedias. An omen if ever an omen existed, but of what?

Some might claim El Dragón's sudden appearance to be the cause, again without proof. How could a dragon be the cause of anything? Unless, of course, dragons actually exist. There can be little doubt that El Dragón became a permanent citizen of El Pozo Negro de Contradicciones, although this has never been proved either. Some even say he was baptized. Certainly he was a cause of additional strife between Eusebio and his wife. Possessing only fins, El Dragón was unable to hold a spoon, and Celestina now had another mouth to feed. When she complained to Eusebio he would tell her, "Quiet, Celestina, I'm teaching him to play dominoes."

"And also to drink aguardiente and smoke cigars," Celestina would answer. "Look at him. He can barely keep his seat from the drunkenness and coughing."

And Eusebio would say, "It's because he's not used to chairs. If you live in the sea then sitting isn't necessary. You can simply swim to the bottom and lie among the corals."

There were other sources of conflict between them, one being El Dragón's flatulence. It seems that dragons, having been raised on diets of fish and seaweed, are unable to process beans. Then there was El Arbol, accompanied everywhere by a black and white dog that relentlessly pissed on his leg, much to Celestina's disgust. Each of these events or situations might have caused what happened next.

All we know is this. One day Modesto rolled into the village of El Pozo Negro de Contradicciones hauling a cargo of straw and turnips. His pants pockets were filled with copper coins, and Angélica's house was to be his first stop. By his calculation the baby would be a month old, eliminating any inconvenience of riding the hump. Beside him on the seat was an unopened bottle of aguardiente, and his shirt pockets were stuffed with cigars. Life would be good, or so he thought.

To his astonishment the village had disappeared. Not a vestige of it remained. The road led not into the commercial section of the banyan where El Seco had his barbershop and Esmeralda her table of trinkets, but through an unfamiliar forest of towering mahogany trees. Eusebio's path had disappeared too, into a wall of mangroves.

Modesto got down from his cart and peered over and under the branches, seeing that the boat was gone. In panic he waded among the roots, coming at last to a few tattered strands of rope. If the boat had sunk the pieces would still be there, but the mud all around was smooth and undisturbed.

He returned to the former site of the village, thinking that the endless banyan had finally succumbed to loggers, but found himself in primary forest. The great trunks and prop roots had vanished. He wandered around looking for some sign—a cracked pot or bit of clothing, anything—but could find no evidence of human habitation. His thoughts hung in the stillness like hovering birds: how could this be?

When life stalls, if only for an instant, the engine of death accelerates. Had everyone died of a plague? Then where were the bones, the graves? Nowhere. He climbed onto his cart and opened the bottle of aguardiente. Darkness began painting in the shadows. Images that a moment before had been branches descended suddenly from the trees, rocks sprang from the ground, lianas strained and creaked at their moorings. From up and down imagined alleys and rutted paths came ghostly voices, the night sounds of people closing their ears to the sounds of night.

At the Drive-in with Monk and His Minions

MONK'S JUST COME BACK from fighting niggers over in Logan where they grow them really mean and now his eyebrows don't line up anymore. His nose is also crooked and split, but that might be from another time. Buddy tells him he looks like shit, maybe worse. Nobody except Buddy would dare say this to Monk, but Buddy has a different way of insulting people and mostly he gets away with it. If Buddy were a dog he'd be grinning and lolling his tongue around and rolling over on his back and baring his scrotum as if saying, it's me, Buddy, and I'm only kidding.

Monk somehow understands this and admits that he maybe feels a little like shit. Like shit warmed over. Monk shakes his head as if the joke's on him and then spits out some blood that looks black under the street lamp. "Tooth," he says, tapping the side of his jaw. "Makes two this week. Fuckin niggers."

We nod sympathetically, even Oliver who's a nigger himself but one of ours. He isn't related to anybody over in Logan or even through Long Bottom or anywhere along the road that leads to Logan. "Sumbitches," Oliver says.

It's a hot Friday night in August. There's nothing to do in the coal camp. Not that there's anything happening on a cold night in

87

January either. Grady, Buddy's kid brother, is throwing a rubber ball against the side of a tree. The ball is little and red like those balls that girls use when they sit on the floor and play jax. Grady is running all over the place because with the trunk of the tree being cylindrical and wrapped in ragged bark the return bounce is unpredictable. Alvin stands with arms folded grinning like the fool he is, legs spread in saw-horse position, a baseball cap pulled low over his eyes. Alvin believes that he is cute because the girls all think so and once in a great while a homely one tells him this to his face. Everyone calls him Junebug. When Alvin was a baby his older sister would say, "Alvin, you are cute as a Junebug," and the name stuck. At least that's what Alvin says, not that people can really remember what happens to them when they're babies.

Like moths, we seem drawn to the single lamp where wings are beaten and tattered mindlessly. In its false brightness what beauty we see in ourselves and others is illusory, like the flat dimensions of stones revealed by their slanted shadows. The camp suddenly darkens. It's eight o'clock and Mr. Browning has just turned out the lights in the company store. He's also turned off the street lamp. Huff Creek tinkles and hisses blackly over stones, protesting confinement. As if light muffles sound we now hear water sliding invisibly as blood through an artery. Katydids hidden in the grass and a whippoorwill off in the dark mountains make their place-sounds.

Other lights beckon now, another choice of a resting place for dusty brittle bodies where our wasted forms will lie heaped beneath an artificial sun manufactured by Hollywood. We're ready. The time is ours and it's right to find a new lamp, shed some wing scales somewhere.

The air seems strangely softened. With the light nearly gone the world has become feminine. In a darkening of desire the whole of the crepuscular sky has grown horns, the floating moon wears lace panties. Treetops black and crinkled swish in the wind, the woods itself creeps closer, earthy and damp and warm, scented with a lingering musk. Out somewhere creatures are mating. Ezra, who hasn't spoken within our short span of collective memory, speaks now: "Let's get some moonshine and go to the drive-in."

"Ooooooooh!" howls Junebug, lifting his chin. He's baying at the moon now edged over the mountains from Kentucky where they've recently cut loose its string.

Feet shuffle as if going somewhere, but nobody actually moves, no one is leaning one direction or another. Group decisions need a moment or two; we're not truly herd animals, not horses that stampede off in a single direction when the leader or maybe another horse spooks. And so we laze around, each one sniffing the air and thinking his own thoughts. Ezra takes from his shirt pocket a pouch of Bull Durham and some rolling papers and starts rolling a smoke. We bum papers from him and take a pinch of two of tobacco and roll smokes for ourselves. When nobody has any matches the cigarettes are stuck behind ears, right or left depending on preference or handedness, where in either case an abundance of hair grease turns them transparent as frog spawn.

Grady starts throwing his ball at the tree again, but it's nearly dark and in chasing it around he bumps into Monk, who cuffs him. Buddy sees this. He knows that Monk will likely stomp Grady's ass just because no one has any matches and Monk is pissed because he'd really like a good smoke after a hard day of fighting niggers. Like a killdeer, one of those sandpipers that builds its nest on open ground and fakes being crippled to lure away predators, Buddy lures Monk away from Grady. "Hey, Monk," he says, "I think I'll whup your ugly self," and he takes off at a lope. Monk knows he can't catch Buddy, who runs track at the high school, so he makes a half-hearted swipe at Grady and laughs.

"How much we got?" Ezra asks. We dig deep and huddle around bumping shoulders and jostling. Change clanks onto crumpled macadam and we drop in unison to paw for it blindly.

"Shit," Junebug says, "I think I dropped fifty cents. Y'all cover me?"

"You never done owned fifty cents," Ezra says unkindly. "White trash like yourself?"

"You got no right to say that," replies Junebug and punches Ezra in the shoulder, hard. Ezra's change falls to the ground.

"Goddammit, 'Bug," Ezra says, bending over, but Junebug only laughs. We find there's enough to buy a quart of moonshine and also get into the drive-in. The moonshine will cost two dollars, the drive-in seventy-five cents for the driver and car and fifty cents a person after that. Some people try hiding on the floor or in the trunk to get in free, but the drive-in manager knows every trick. He makes you open the trunk and shines a flashlight around under your feet. We just want in, that's all.

Ezra has his daddy's car, a '54 Plymouth now five years old with matching streaks of mud up both sides and a few stringy squirrel tails tied to the antenna. The thing has seen some wear with Ezra's daddy and uncle driving it to the mines every day. His daddy tried seat covers at first, but nothing saved those seats. No matter where you sit when you get in there's coal dust on you when you get out.

We pile in with Ezra driving, me in the middle, and Monk riding shotgun. In the back are Buddy, Grady, Junebug, and Oliver. "Your granny still got that good white liquor?" Ezra asks, searching in the rearview mirror for Oliver's face.

"She got it," Oliver replies. Everyone knew that Miz Wain, Oliver's grandma, was a moonshiner. She sold it by the mason jar and expected you to supply your own. You could take a little and slosh it around in the bottom of the jar first if you wanted, but no ring of foam ever formed at the edges. Miz Wain never added kerosene or anything like that to her product. Her stuff sometimes made people go temporarily blind and it often made them so sick they wished they were dead, but nobody ever got poisoned or died. Miz Wain was a good Christian lady and she wouldn't have wanted that on her conscience. You heard her voice rising above the others from the little church where the niggers went every Sunday. You could hear the choir when you walked down off the mountain to collect spring water. They'd be singing and clapping and stomping their feet and hollering like the Lord himself was about to set them down some-place else that probably looked about like where they were standing.

From the parking lot in front of the company store we take a dirt road that runs parallel to the train tracks. At the crossing Ezra downshifts and bumps over onto another road more rutted than the first. This road is perpendicular to the tracks and begins a few hundred feet beyond the last house in the camp. It leads into Nigger Holler, unofficial name of the nigger community whose adult male members work the same mines and perform the same jobs as the white men who live in the camp. The houses there are mostly unpainted shacks, little worse than our company houses. According to Monk a nigger never paints his house for fear that a lazier nigger neighbor will get insulted. Nobody has ever pointed out to Monk that our own houses also lack paint.

We pull into the yard of a shack and Oliver jumps out. "Y'all wait here," he says, then asks, "Any you dumb-ass white boys got a mason jar?"

"Do I look like I got one on me?" Buddy asks.

"No, the only thing you got on you is ugliness of the face," Oliver answers. Meanwhile Ezra is rummaging under the front seat.

"No jars here," he reports to Oliver, who has come around to the driver's side and is leaning partway into the car through the open window.

"Shit," Oliver says disgustedly. He takes the ever-present toothpick out of his mouth and shakes his head. Ezra hands him two dollars collected from all of us and he bounds up onto the porch. Oliver is a halfback on the football team and he's lithe and quick. While we watch expectantly Oliver has second thoughts and returns and asks me to go along so his grandma won't think the liquor is just for him.

I can picture the scene inside. I was there once before with Oliver. I see a front room with little knickknacks everywhere and doilies on the furniture. Against one wall is an iron stove that burns both wood and coal. Off to each side is a bedroom. Oliver sleeps in one and his sister and their grandma in the other. The kitchen is the room at the back pressed up against the base of the mountain. To get to the outhouse you go through the kitchen door. Under the kitchen sink is a spigot sticking through a hole in the back wall of the house. The spigot is connected to a garden hose, which is connected to dozens of other garden hoses that snake up the side of the mountain into the woods where Miz Wain has her still. Over in the camp we can sometimes smell the sour odor of fermenting corn. Miz Wain doesn't keep any liquor in the house out of respect for Jesus Christ Our Lord and Savior.

Inside is what I remember from before. The room is crowded with furniture, some of it cloth-covered and patched. Everything is clean as can be except the cracks in the floor, which can never be made clean with a dust mop. The walls are lined with pictures of Miz Wain's late husband and of Oliver and his sister and interspersed are framed embroidered homilies on the sweetness of home and confirmation in bright thread that Jesus loves everybody. A large calico cat looks up from an armchair. It yawns and stretches sleepily in the manner of cats, arching its back and poking out some claws.

Miz Wain waddles into the kitchen with Oliver following and then me. She kneels like a groaning camel in front of the sink and fills a quart mason jar of her own. She smiles graciously and says that a fifteen-cent deposit is necessary to guarantee the jar will be returned. For a quarter she'll sell the jar. I hand over a quarter knowing this jar will never survive tonight. Oliver leans against the wall digging the toothpick around in his molars, one leg crossed over the other. After the money changes hands he grunts, untangles himself, and gives his grandma a kiss on the cheek.

Monk opens the door and gets out so I can again sit in the middle. He likes riding shotgun because he can yell insults directly out the window without having to lean over someone else. "First," Monk says, "we need matches." This attempt at enumeration ends quickly; there are no second or third directives. It's about as much as we can deal with anyway with everyone's mind stuck on a single subject.

Ezra turns the radio up full volume and we bump back through the parking lot of the company store and take the one-lane bridge over Huff Creek and onto the hard road, stopping at a bar to get a pack of matches. Everyone lights up including Grady, who is thirteen. I turn around to check out the backseat and notice Junebug watching Grady with the interest of an entomologist studying a caterpillar.

Junebug digs his elbow into Grady's side making him wince and start coughing. "Gettin any?" Junebug asks maliciously.

"Leave him alone," Buddy says.

"You stick with me tonight, young feller, if you want to pick up some pussy," Junebug says confidently. "Them girls all love me to pieces."

"You ain't ever been up close to pussy," Buddy retorts, answering for his brother. "Now leave him alone."

Junebug grins and his white teeth flash in the light of a passing car. "Y'all keep your eyes on the 'Bug. He'll lead you to the Promised Land."

"He'll lead you to step in a pile of dog shit," Ezra says. Everyone laughs, but nothing shakes Junebug's confidence where girls are concerned. He's the most stuck-up person ever.

"Oliver," Monk says, "pass forward that jar of corn squeezins." Monk takes a healthy sip and rolls it around in his mouth to cauterize the memory hole of his tooth, then swallows hard. "Hot *damn!*" he says.

He passes the jar to me. I take a sip and make an appropriate comment of approval before passing the jar to Ezra, who takes his hands off the steering wheel momentarily causing the car to weave over the white line. Miz Wain's product is almost pure alcohol, and the fire is unbelievable. "Oh my!" Ezra exclaims when he can regain his breath. "Keep that away from my poor old momma and baby sisters, 'cause it would shorely lead them into sin." Someone in the back says amen and Ezra hands the jar over his shoulder.

Junebug digs into Grady's ribs again. "Hey, chillun, you gonna get your ass paddled by Mr. Adkins?" Grady would be starting eighth grade in the fall. We laugh and hoot. Everyone knew about Mr. Adkins and his famous paddle. Sooner or later he got almost every boy in woodworking. If you talked or fooled around on the lathe or didn't sweep up the shop floor just right you were called to the front. Then Mr. Adkins would say, "Okay, boy, drop 'em and let's get on with it." While the victim dropped his drawers to reveal tattered skivvies—or sometimes no skivvies—Mr. Adkins reached under his desk and withdrew a paddle almost as long as his arm. After instructing the boy to grip the edge of the table saw and present his rear end, Mr. Adkins stood his paddle on the concrete floor and leaned the handle against his thigh. He bent at the waist and spit on his hands for a better grip, mimicking Duke Snyder of the Dodgers when he's waiting in the on-deck circle except that Mr. Adkins is squat and dim of eye and bats right-handed. Finally, after a delicious pause, he pronounced the sentence: "Three licks." And there the victim stood trembling, his ass glowing sweetly in the fluorescent lights, considering for probably the first time in his short life the consequence of the revolution lost.

"Oh, mercy!" Buddy exclaims after taking his first swallow.

"You remember that paddle?" Junebug asks nobody in particular. We all yell in assent except Monk who saw it almost daily during his brief tenure in junior high.

"All painted and varnished like furniture," Ezra says.

"And the *holes* in it," Junebug adds while looking down at Grady. "They say them holes increase the vo-*loss*-ity and gives it a bigger sting. I wonder how your skinny little ass is gonna survive."

It was true that when Mr. Adkins paddled you there was soreness for a week or more, but it made you a hero in the halls. The girls took notice and giggled when you walked by, and they giggled even more upon watching you sit down carefully on those hard classroom chairs.

Buddy reaches across Grady and hands the jar to Junebug. "Say, boy, you done forgot your kin," Junebug says, and he hands the jar to Grady.

"Don't give him none," Buddy says, slightly alarmed. "He's too little."

"I can take it," Grady says, and he tips back the jar and swallows long and hard, a longer swallow than any of us would venture. Immediately he coughs and chokes and his eyes tear up, but he keeps it down.

"Good shit, huh boy?" Ezra says, looking in the rearview mirror. "Make you a man." Grady nods enthusiastically, but he doesn't seem to mean it.

Junebug tips the jar and swallows. "Oh Lordy," he says. "That is some good 'shine, no offence, Oliver."

"Gimme the damn jar," Oliver says. He sounds grouchy. When I turn to ask him why he's in such a crappy mood he doesn't answer, but I can tell he's had a sip by the grimace on his face. Oliver always takes his swallows stoically, not commenting on the quality of the product, probably because he isn't the sort to brag and carry on about kin.

Oliver taps Monk on the shoulder, which is a signal for Monk to reach his hand back to receive the jar. Junebug pipes up and says, "Hey Monk, I thought you didn't drink after niggers."

Monk turns in the seat and says, "Watch your mouth, 'Bug, 'cause Oliver ain't a nigger and I got no problem drinkin after him."

"I just seen his lips on the rim of that jar," says Junebug, "and they looked somewhat dark to me."

Monk has turned back and is facing the front again. He says to the windshield, "There's niggers and there's niggers and your too stupid to know the difference."

"Then how come I cain't see the boy unless he smiles?" Junebug replies. He's asking for it. Buddy knows this just like the rest of us and he takes the opportunity to reach over and smack Junebug a good one on the ear.

Junebug returns the favor just as Monk reaches around and lays a short punch on Junebug's jaw. Oliver is loving it all. He's grinning and slapping his hand on his leg and laughing in a high-pitched cackle. Only Oliver laughs like this. You can easily pick out Oliver's laugh in a roomful of laughing people. Meanwhile Monk has handed me the jar and I'm trying hard to keep from spilling it with all the jostling going on.

In no time we're at the drive-in. The movies don't start until dark when people can see the screen clearly. Friday and Saturday nights are triple features and the last movie ends after one o'clock in the morning. This is good because the boys have ample time to visit with their friends and get good and drunk and those with girlfriends or wives can swap some spit and maybe squeeze a little tittie. It isn't unheard of for couples to actually go all the way, but anyone who does is either awfully clever or strangers from out of town. It would be very difficult to get any serious loving with some drunken acquaintance banging on the windshield and hollering, "Say there old son, you got any rollin papers and maybe a little drink on you?"

Mr. Merritt the drive-in manager looks in the car and totes up the amount. He makes Ezra open the trunk, and he shines his light all around inside the car until it comes to rest on the jar of moonshine. Then he aims the light on each of us one at a time and says, "I don't want no trouble, hear me? There's families with little kids and stuff so no fightin." Then he shines the light directly at Monk and adds, "You hear me Monk? I'll be watchin you, boy."

"How about a little sip of corn made personal by Miz Wain?" Ezra says. Ezra is a real politician. He knows we'll have a better time if old Mr. Merritt thinks highly of us.

"Well now thank you, Ezra," says Mr. Merritt, and he accepts the jar and takes a long sip. He wipes his mouth on his sleeve and spits a stream of tobacco juice on the ground. "That's mighty good." He bends down and looks Oliver in the eye and says, "My best to your grandma, boy." Oliver nods and we're through the gate.

We drive around in the back row until we find a speaker that hasn't been ripped off its cord. Buddy gets out and tests it and reports that the sound works fine. Ezra eases the car into the space and rolls his window up a few inches, providing enough glass to support the speaker clip. He turns up the volume, but the movie hasn't yet started and there's nothing but recorded advertising for the concession stand. Whoever made the recording must be from somewhere like New York or Memphis because the accent isn't from around here. Meanwhile Monk is already out the door and walking over to another car where two people are exchanging saliva. When Monk bangs on the roof they unclasp and look around. It's Dallas and Betty Lou. Dallas graduated two years ago and is working the mines; Betty Lou will be a senior with us this year. By us I mean everyone in our car except Grady. And Monk, of course, who's nineteen but never graduated.

Monk opens the back door and sits down leaving his feet sticking out so he can spit easier. The car is one vacant space away and we can hear the subsequent conversation.

"Why if it ain't ol' Monk!" Dallas hollers, turning to shake Monk's hand as if one of them has just been elected mayor. "Have a snort," and he passes over an open fifth of sour mash.

Monk takes a long swallow and reports, "This stuff tastes like R.

C. next to what we got next door. We got some of Miz Wain's home-cooked mash." He hands the bottle back. Dallas grins brownly through bad teeth. It looks like Betty Lou has been chewing on him some because he's wearing a necklace of scabs set in yellowing hematomas.

"Did you hear the news?" Betty Lou asks. Then without waiting for an answer she says, "Me and Dally's gettin married." She leans over and gives Dallas a little nip on the collar bone.

"You don't look knocked up," Monk remarks.

"Well I ain't. We're bein real careful. Right, sugar?" Everyone hoots, including all of us in the next car.

Just then the peripheral floodlights go out and trumpets blare through the speakers announcing that the first feature is about to start. This one will be for the kids. After watching it and visiting the concession stand at intermission they'll fall asleep, maybe restlessly maybe not. For some the backseat will be softer than where they sleep at home and perhaps less crowded.

Monk shows no sign of coming back soon and I slide over into his place. We pass the jar around. The backseat is tight with four so Buddy gets out and comes around and tries to open my door, but I give him a punch in the chest through the open window. He curses and lets go of the door handle. The movie has started, but already the laughter and conversations around us are almost as loud. Buddy invites me to step outside which I do. We throw a couple of punches and scuffle around some, but neither is trying to injure the other. Finally we quit and start to laugh. Oliver gets out and gives the night its first cackle. He's feeling some effects of his grandma's product and probably the rest of us are too. All except Monk, who can drink with the best.

Someone is vomiting. We walk around behind the car and lean against the rear fenders watching Grady puke up his guts. He's too sick even to stagger properly and seems to have gone both blind and mute. Now that I'm also somewhat drunk, images seem discontinuous as if the events are happening someplace else. Flickers of light from the screen have that oddly remote quality of distant starlight and I wonder how many light years away I am from the source, standing here on the hump of a small planet in the spinning universe.

I'm conscious of Oliver's hand on my shoulder, whether in camaraderie or for physical support is uncertain, but he's saying something neither of us understands about his sister or mine.

"What am I gonna do, go with your sisser?" Oliver asks. He lies down in the cinders and looks up. I'm leaning against a speaker post and spreading my legs trying to make a tripod so I don't fall. My sister is twelve.

"My sister's only twelve," I say. Then I shout, "My sister's only twelve!" I see Monk look over then go back to his conversation with Dallas. Betty Lou is watching the movie, a cartoon of some kind, evidently as practice for when she has little kids and brings them to the drive-in.

Oliver rolls his eyes whitely and sits up. "Supposin she was sixteen. I still wouldn't go with her. What could we do, come to the drive-in? Ha! You think Monk and Alvin and them other hillbillies wouldn't beat the shit out of me?" He lies down again, the back of his head once more in cinders.

"I wouldn't go with yours either," I reply, but I say it with less conviction. Oliver's sister is sixteen and looks like she's been dipped in light milk chocolate. She's got a sly smile and titties that stretch past hope in the average fuzzy sweater. Her legs aren't any darker than a tanned white girl's and better shaped than any I've ever seen even in a girlie magazine. There I was the last day of school standing in front of my locker when she sauntered over like slow dancing, swaying back and forth, big brown eyes focused on my chest. She was burdened by an armload of books clasped against her and when she got so close I could see every individual hair on her head and smell her perfume she looked up gradually and open-eyed and flashed those white teeth and banged me with a hip and whispered, "You are the *finest* boy in this school." As she walked away she looked over her shoulder and tilted back her head and laughed. I didn't know what to think, but taking a short bark at some moon was a possibility, if there had been one handy.

"That's good," Oliver said, "because if y'all get married where would you live? How'd you take to bein the only hillbilly in Nigger Holler? And you think your momma and daddy would let my baby sisser move in wit' y'all? Ha!" It was definitely something to consider when I sobered up. I couldn't remember wanting to marry Oliver's sister, but maybe I did. She was prettier and smarter than any of the blonde vixens who strode the halls looking past you, just a shade darker.

"Then you won't quit my sisser 'cause she's a Negro?" Oliver is sitting up again, but his eyes are unsteady on mine, or maybe mine on his. Things have become very confusing. Were Alice and I going together? Wouldn't I know it if we were?

"Hey Buddy!" I yell across the roof of the car. "Do Alice and I go together?" Suddenly my back slips away from the speaker pole. Tripod sprung, I collapse sprawling in the cinders. From this new vantage point I see a human form under the car, although it doesn't seem to be anyone I know.

"Alice who?" comes the reply.

"Oliver's baby sister," I say.

"Not unless you're a nigger lover," Buddy answers from somewhere in space. His voice sounds smaller after having been filtered through multiple layers of metal and upholstery.

"See?" I say to Oliver as if in confirmation. Of what I'm not sure.

Junebug has arrived and hands me the jar of moonshine. I take a drink and pass it to Oliver. Junebug is drunk. I can tell from the sort of smirk he wears when he's had too much.

"I thought we were friends," says Oliver morosely, "and now you're quittin my baby sisser. She's really crazy about you."

I was stunned. This beautiful and enticing girl was crazy about *me*? I wasn't vain enough to be insulted just because Alice is black. I sit back against the speaker pole and try this on for fit.

"Then I won't quit her," I say.

Oliver scoots over on his knees and grabs my right hand and pumps it up and down. "You promise?"

"Sure," I reply, not at all certain what I had just said, but not regretting it a whole lot either. Alice and me together? Anything is credible when you're drunk. Nothing appears outright stupid or impossible, not in the company of friends and the flickering movie light and the cinders soft and surprisingly comfortable.

"I thought you didn't want me to go with Alice," I say, suddenly lucid. But Oliver has become distracted by a fight that has broken out several rows in front.

"Who's fightin?" Buddy asks. He's come around from the other side of the car.

"Some ol' boys from Davis," Junebug replies. "They're dumb-asses, ain't they?" Oliver hands him the jar.

"I thought you didn't drink after niggers," Buddy says and starts to laugh.

"Naw," Junebug answers, tipping the jar, "that's Monk. And Monk says Oliver here is a white man so I got no problem."

Oliver cackles and stretches out in the cinders. "If you be the typical white man, then I'm happy bein a Negro," he says. We pass the jar all around again even to Ezra who gets so quiet when he drinks you would think he's off on Mars or maybe Jupiter, body and mind. Grady has conked out on the cinders with his head underneath the car. It's his form I saw. At Buddy's suggestion we pull him out by his ankles and throw him in the backseat like a sack of scratch corn. He smells pretty bad because after he vomited he fell down in it and rolled around.

"That'll learn him," Junebug chuckles.

"Goddammit 'Bug, now leave him alone!" Buddy has become irrational about protecting his baby brother and in this instance I'm inclined to side with Junebug. After all you can't really niggle at someone who is unconscious. Buddy hauls off and pops Junebug a good one directly between the dimples. Fortunately it's Ezra who is holding the jar and not Junebug or for sure the contents would now be soaking into the cinders leaving us no choice except to go around bumming drinks from friends for two more full-length features.

Junebug isn't one to turn the other cheek. He pops Buddy right back and now they're scratching and punching like they mean to kill one another and maybe they would except Monk gets out of Dallas' car and breaks it up. They're both bloody and scratched up from the cinders, which really aren't that soft against the cheek if another person is attempting to grind your face into them.

At intermission Junebug goes to the concession stand to look for girls, who often come to the drive-in in groups, several in one car. That's the last we see of him tonight. Dallas gets out and goes too. Betty Lou drinks lots of R. C. Colas and eats the occasional chocolate Moon Pie and he needs to keep her supplied through the second feature.

———————

To this day neither Oliver nor I can remember the names of those movies. For thirty-seven years we've tried, but nothing clicks. Oliver looks the part of a Washington lawyer, graying at the temples, slim in a dark suit. He leans back and clasps hands behind his head and squints up at the Lincoln Memorial. "I've got it!" he cackles. His hands drop and his body snaps forward. "The second feature was *She Wore a Yellow Ribbon* with John Wayne. That's it!"

"No chance," I reply. "That came out years earlier. I remember seeing that movie at the drive-in with my parents when I was a very little kid."

Oliver looks morose but quickly regains his smile. "Oh well, good try. Anyhow, if we ever figured it out, what would we have in common?" I laugh and Oliver cackles and we unwrap our sandwiches. It's a sunny day in spring, a good day to be at the Mall. The air is warm in the sun, chilly in the shade, as yet devoid of the odors of sweltering summer. Joggers wearing grim expressions huff past. We're sitting on a bench underneath the trees where we meet once a week and later we'll walk over to the Vietnam Memorial to pay respects to an old friend whose fate was perhaps determined by events of that night at the drive-in.

I awoke the next morning on Miz Wain's couch in shimmering coolness where the ceiling lath spun like a raft overhead. Porous curtains pulled shut and anchored at the bottom filled and collapsed, breathing with the autonomic rhythm of lungs. The doors to the other rooms were closed. I was dirty all over from lying in cinders, from scuffling against the mud-wrapped car. My mouth tasted of bile, but I didn't remember puking. In fact I remembered very little, even how I came to be where I was. I lay quietly intending to get up and leave, when a door opened and Alice stepped into the room. She was barefoot, wearing a short nightgown, her hair pulled back into a fuzzy ponytail and tied with a ribbon, and when she smiled I was stunned by her beauty.

She walked softly to the couch and sat on the edge, pushing her hip gently against mine until I scooted over. Her lower lip slid between her teeth for just a moment. The gesture seemed coquettish, irresistible, and I think now that love might start simply as a mosaic of appealing mannerisms, enduring until we tire of them or die. "Feelin better, shortcakes?" she asked. I remember her kisses on my cheek and neck, on my lips very softly, and then she whispered, "You are mine, you know, and don't ever forget." I never did.

There naturally followed taunts of nigger lover, the threats of cross burnings in my parents' yard, and in school someone occasionally asked if my dues to the Klan were paid up, but all told things went smoothly.

Like a dream incompletely unrealized the year 1959 lies cracked and faded in memory, drab predecessor of the masturbatory '60s when a whole generation of narcissists fell prostrate upon seeing its composite image reflected back from a pool of K-Y Jelly. Oliver and I emerged largely unscathed from that decade of protest and confusion. For this we offer thanks; for the myth of the conscious being we are only sad. Every life seems shrouded in fog and if we emerge at all it's for a few pellucid moments, time enough to view each other with prejudice and fear before retreating.

Yesterday evening we were shopping for groceries, all of us. Alice was walking ahead carrying a family-size box of Cheerios pressed against her chest like it might have been a book. She turned suddenly and faced me, biting her lower lip and swaying to a rhythm no one else could hear. She slow-danced around the shopping cart and gave me the hip. She's still slim and beautiful; she still has those designer legs. "You know," she said, looking at the buttons of my shirt and opening one of them ever so slightly, "you are the *finest* boy in this supermarket." Our two teenage sons exchanged glances and rolled their eyes. "Ma," the older one said, "please behave."

Oliver went off to Grambling on a football scholarship. Afterward, riding partly on the greased skids of Affirmative Action, he was accepted into Georgetown Law and eventually took a job with the Department of Commerce. While in law school he married a white classmate, who currently has a lucrative practice with a private firm. Both our families live comfortably in Arlington.

In the '50s it was customary for Southern judges to give troublemakers the option of serving jail time or joining the military. This choice was presented to Monk a week or so following our night at the drive-in. While Dallas was standing in line at the concession stand Monk had gotten into the front seat and bitten a large hickey on Betty Lou's neck, at the same time taking the opportunity to squeeze some tittie. This behavior Betty Lou reported angrily to Dallas upon his return, leading to ugly words and the most vicious fight anyone had seen in years. Monk broke Dallas' nose and was bashing his face repeatedly into the concrete base of a speaker pole when Mr. Merritt and some other men finally arrived to pull him away, snarling and biting and clawing like a wild animal. Dallas spent two weeks in the hospital with a serious concussion, not to mention numerous stitches. His nose healed, although it never again resembled a human nose, and Betty Lou, ever a believer in Lamarckian evolution, worried that her future children might now inherit Dallas' new nose instead of the old one.

We all showed up the day Monk left for Parris Island, seeing him off at the bus station. Already there was talk of another war in Asia and Monk assured us he was ready to help hold back the yellow hordes now poised to storm American shores. It was time the gooks got a real ass-kicking. All he asked was the opportunity, and he figured the Marines would be into it before anybody. He said he was ready, that fighting gooks was no different from fighting niggers except you got to shoot the sumbitches and Uncle Sam paid you for it. We waited until the Greyhound turned out of sight then spent the rest day in a bar shooting pool.

Junebug and Ezra went into the mines after graduation; I moved eighty miles up the road to the state university. Alice followed the next year. I earned a degree in biology and presently edit copy in a basement office of the National Marine Fisheries Service. Alice graduated in civil engineering and also works for the government. We'll retire vested bureaucrats.

Every Wednesday, rain or shine, Oliver and I leave a red rose at the Vietnam Memorial. If he knew he'd probably tell us we were a couple of queers who needed to be drop-kicked in the balls. Still, we do it. Memorials celebrate the living; the dead have no memory and express no desire to be remembered. Somewhere inside that polished black stone crouches an image that faintly eludes, not the one of rice paddies and leeches and napalm, but of a boy somebody said once looked like a monkey, jug-eared and tough. The Marines taught him teamwork, how to march in step, to fight only when ordered to fight. His eighty-pound pack must have fit him like a saddle.

Home on leave before a second tour Monk said, "The birds sound different in 'Nam. They don't have whippoorwills over there." Those words came out indifferently as he stood among us erect and un-moving, the warrior stallion at rest, mouthing the bit loosely where teeth once fit as if awaiting only a sharp sting of spurs in the ribs. He seemed aloof to death, disdainful of its pettiness and squalor. He seemed to us like Christ.

Old Woman
Framed and Backlit

WE CAME TOGETHER ON a cold night of tenuous wind. Trees swayed blackly overhead and snow lay in glittering screes against the curbs. Dusty snowflakes had collected like dander on the shoulders of her tattered coat. The stoop, the shuffling steps made her seem ancient. Her hair had recently been wet. It was matted, the ends straight and frozen.

"I've been waiting for you," she said in a voice without reproach or complaint.

"I meant to come sooner," I replied, and led her to my rooms across the street.

Once inside the building, I helped her along the dim corridor, careful to see that her shoes, which were sturdy and of an antiquated design, did not catch in the threadbare carpet. The hall was narrow. When we reached my door I nudged her gently toward the opposite wall so I could insert the key into the lock.

After stepping inside I beckoned her to follow. She hesitated, framed in the doorway and backlit, her face in shadow. "Is this correct?" she asked.

"Yes," I answered.

"Then we can begin." Without further hesitation she stepped across the threshold. I switched on my desk lamp, and when I turned again to face her she was blinking back the light. Her eyes were two black coals set in a furrowed face, her lips like the orifice of a damp internal organ exposed suddenly to the dry air.

"May I take your coat?"

"No, I'll keep it. On such a cold night a person can't warm up properly even indoors."

"Please sit down," I said, indicating an armchair beside my desk. She was short—tiny, actually—and when she sat her feet did not quite reach the floor giving her the strange appearance of a wizened child.

I took off my own coat and scarf, shook away the snow, and hung them behind the door. I shucked my wet boots by forcing heel to toe. My wool socks were damp, but not wet, and would soon dry in the heat of the room.

"At last," I said, sitting down at the desk and picking up notebook and pencil. I scraped the chair around to face her. "Sorry for the delay."

"No apology is necessary," she replied evenly. The slight lisp in her speech and the mannerism of working her lips continuously as if sucking on a straw were probably caused by ill-fitting false teeth. I made a quick note, hoping my observation had been surreptitious.

"My false teeth don't fit right," she said, just as I finished writing. "They told me down at the clinic I could get them fixed, or maybe the state would buy me new ones. But I don't want new ones. Too many trips downtown on the bus to see the dentist. I'd rather keep these."

"I'm sure you can do what you want." My low lamp forced a circle of light onto the desk top. The light of a neon sign across the street blinked weakly through the window behind me, and it was now I who was backlit. Except for a digital clock on the kitchen counter, everything was in shadow.

"I haven't yet put this into my story," I said. "Would you feel better if I didn't?"

"No, why should I care whether you mention false teeth? I'm an old woman, vanity means nothing to me now. Once I was young and beautiful, and when I walked on the beach at Atlantic City the boys trailed along like a pack of hounds. I was always coming out of the sea and pushing back my hair. I dripped water everywhere. They joked and said I must be a mermaid and that soon my hair would turn green as seaweed, my legs would become a fish's tail. The boys told me this long ago. I can't remember their faces, just their words. Everyone grows old, maybe even mermaids."

"Excuse me," I said and wrote furiously for several minutes, trying to remember her words verbatim. "That was quite a soliloquy," I remarked when I had finished. "And quite an intimate one, after a fashion."

"What?"

"Quite a speech. I've never heard you reveal so much about yourself," I continued, regretting these words at once. "But please don't stop. I need your words and memories."

"I know," she sighed. "But your writing adds things. . .lies, half-truths. You add to what I say and make me into someone I'm not."

"My imagination does that," I explained. "It dilutes reality with a measure of unreality, guiding human experience onto another level."

She shook her head. "I can't think about those things from my youth. They shred the few memories I have left. Now you've replaced those with others and stuck them inside me until I'm not me any longer. I can feel you writing me, and your sentences are like alien fingers inside my chest squeezing my heart."

I set down my pencil and leaned back. There was a moment's pause while she pulled at the ends of a faded shawl tied loosely under her chin. "You're a. . .a parasite sucking out my memories and leaving nothing except a shell." Her mouth was working furiously. She grasped the chair arms and pushed herself back, thinking perhaps that she was again sitting in a rocker.

"It can't be helped," I said, hoping not to sound too abrupt. I consulted my notebook, leafing through the pages until finding the right one. "Your sister was killed by a car when you were six or seven, you don't remember exactly. This sister was your identical twin, and her death left you divided, as if a part of yourself had died too." I tapped the page with my finger to reinforce its veracity. When I looked up she was watching me. Tears formed, one in each coal-black eye, and coursed in synchrony down the furrows of her face.

"My sister drowned," she said. "We were playing by the river. Her body was never found. I don't recall any car accident. If it happened, I wasn't there."

"The story is clear," I insisted. "I've written it. We're here tonight to sort out a few remaining details and inconsistencies. So if you'll bear with me I can send you along home shortly. The last bus stops on the corner at one forty-five."

I settled back and consulted the notebook again. My writing was difficult to read in the dimness, and I turned away from her to better illuminate the pages.

"You and your sister—you've never mentioned her name—were playing on the sidewalk in front of your house. It was summer, an evening in summer, July maybe. There was a crab apple tree in your front yard, and by your recollection it wasn't in bloom.

"The sultriness is what you recall best, that and insect sounds. And neighborhood noises, of course. Yours was a lower middle class neighborhood, and people had left their windows and doors open for ventilation. You remember laughter. Radios. It was that silvery hour of dusk, no longer light but not dark either, the hour when human vision is impaired by insufficient contrast between objects— even moving objects—and the background.

"Your sister said, 'Let's cross the street,' but you refused. You stood stubbornly on the sidewalk looking down at a pair of dirty bare feet, elbows locked, hands clasped behind you, torso twisting negatively back and forth.

"No!" you shouted. And you repeated it: "No!" Your sister, always the braver one, the leader, went anyway. Upon reaching the other sidewalk she turned to taunt you.

"Your anger and frustration rose. In addition, you felt afraid of being left alone, even in front of your own house. Afraid and ashamed of being afraid. And so you could not give in and relinquish this tiny scrap of independence gained at so great a price. It was a triumph of sorts, a coming out.

"Your sister sensed she had lost control over you and dashed into the street intent on dragging you back across with her, if necessary. In her rage she didn't see the car, which appeared suddenly, its headlights not yet turned on. The driver had no time to brake. He told the police he thought he had struck a dog. You watched the scene in horror, not understanding but somehow knowing your life had changed forever.

"With passing years the event assumed a surreal quality in which certain physical elements became embellished in memory—the flaxen head of your sister lying on the pavement, white now in the dusk, the parents' wrenching grief, the odd juxtaposition of tears splashing on the dark fenders of the very instrument of death.

"Later you were asked why you had *let* your sister cross the street alone, the dominance hierarchies of children having been ignored, if considered at all. A reasonable question from an adult's perspective, one placing guilt and shame squarely where they were thought to belong. Couldn't you have taken charge *just once* to avert a tragedy?

"This is all true," I concluded, "because I made it so. Truths and lies evade the permanence of memory with equal facility.

"My story therefore begins, 'She hesitated, framed in the door-way and backlit, her face invisible.' How do you like it?"

I turned back anticipating a response, but the chair was empty. On the floor before it stood a puddle of water. Sunlight streamed through the open window. From the street came smells and sounds of summer. My boots were nowhere in sight, and when I looked behind the door the coat and scarf were not there either.

Hatchery Life

EVERY TIME IT RAINS I have pH problems and Mr. Owensworth comes out of his office yelling. We have automatic monitoring here at Hatchery. Mr. Owensworth can read the dials from where he's sitting at his desk, sipping Jack Daniel's with his hand up underneath Ms. Swisher's dress. That's his main job as Hatchery Manager, reading the dials. When Mr. Owensworth yells right in your face his breath is so bad you think of the time a raccoon fell into the main sump and drowned. Whew-eee! That was something, let me tell you.

Hatchery is up in the mountains and we still have some hillbillies around. They come down from their shacks on Saturday nights to shop at Wal-Mart. Later they sit in the beds of their pickups and swap hillbilly stories, maybe dip a little Chattanooga Chew Chew and guzzle corn liquor.

The Revenuers don't care anymore what happens to the corn. They have an air-conditioned office over at the Mall. Inside it there's cable TV, cordless phones, and a fax machine connected to Headquarters. The Revenuers are after bigger game, namely Indians selling cigarettes on their reservations. There aren't any Indians around here, just the occasional hillbilly, as I said. Our Revenuers don't do much. They stand more for tradition than anything else.

After a rain the pH of the hatchery water drops and the trout get nervous and fidgety. Then I have to douse the intake system with sodium carbonate to raise the pH back to normal before they jump out of their tanks and end up on the ground. A dead trout is a lost sale. Too many of them and Mr. Owensworth gets a bad sales/Survival Ratio Score in his Personnel Evaluation from Home Office. When that happens he takes it out on us.

My title is Hatcheryman Fourth Class, which is slightly above Fifth Class, and, as you might suspect, somewhat below Third Class. I have a way to go before promotion, but that day will never come so long as Mr. Owensworth is here. He hates me even though Ms. Swisher is my sister. She's supposed to be his secretary, but she's really his You-Know-What. Now that she's important she tells me I can't call her Marlene anymore. According to a Memorandum from Mr. Owensworth, the Staff has to call her Ms. Swisher, and Marlene (pardon me, Ms. Swisher) says the Memorandum included me along with everybody else.

Ms. Swisher's "promotion" has actually been harder on Charlene than on me. They used to be good friends—skipping school and hanging out at the Mall getting matching tattoos, dyeing their hair purple and having it spiked. . .you know, the stuff girlfriends do together. Now Marlene (sorry, I can't help calling her that) sneaks over to the Sunrise Surprise Motel to be with Mr. Owensworth, where they You-Know-What until the wee hours. Around the Office they talk in code so his wife won't suspect anything if she happens to stop by.

Charlene's my fiancée. She goes to the Mall by herself these days. She sits on one of the wooden benches near the Food Court and cries. She tells me it's tough missing the good times with Ms. Swisher and that it's even tougher trying to eat a plate of fries while sobbing your heart out, especially when it's loaded up with ketchup. Then she tells me how hard it is to look at the tattoo on her left triceps that says Recovering Slut because it reminds of Ms. Swisher's.

Sometimes she can't stand it and has to go shopping over at Ye Olde Tattoo Parlour, which is located conveniently across from the Food Court. She picks out a nice design and has the Tattooist apply it wherever he can still find some vacant skin. Right now that's mainly on her butt. I'm trying to be supportive but wonder what will happen when she runs out of available space. Yesterday she showed me her latest, E.T. with his hand out and Tiny Tim sitting in it.

Today we lost five trout to low pH: a brownie, two rainbows, and two brookies. They can't have been dead long because their colors still hadn't faded completely. I was fixing to take them home, maybe have Charlene roll them in a little cornmeal and fry them for supper. Then Mr. Owensworth comes around and says, what are you up to now, stealing trout? I say no, it's low pH the same as always after a big thunderstorm. That's when acid rain falling in the Mountains comes sluicing down through the hollows and right into Number Two Stream, our primary source of influent water.

Mr. Owensworth says horseshit, I recognize a thief when I see one, and you're one. He means a thief. Hand over the trout, he says, and he takes them away and puts them in his office Frigidaire. I know what happens next even before it happens. After doing You-Know-What over at the Sunrise Surprise Motel, Ms. Swisher gets out of bed in the Altogether and puts on a frilly little apron and rolls those trout in cornmeal and fries them up for fat old Mr. Owensworth. I know because Charlene and Ms. Swisher used to share recipes. They both bought copies of "A Hundred Ways to Fry a Trout" at the bookstore in the Mall.

On the way back to his office Mr. Owensworth turns and says, and another thing, you moron, I won't have a thief working a responsible job here at Hatchery. Starting right now you're busted down to Offalman Third Class. He doesn't have to say anything more. It's the lowest position in the Offal Department, which is the lowest department at Hatchery.

Later I try to contact Ms. Swisher and maybe get her on my side so she can sweet-talk Mr. Owensworth. I call her on the intercom but she hangs up. If I tell Charlene about my demotion she'll probably move out. I have a suspicion that Charlene and her Tattooist have something going on. I hope I'm wrong about this because I really love Charlene and I think she loves me back. I can't afford to be fired. If I do it's back to operating the little Merry-Go-Round outside the Food Court. I'll say one thing about that Tattooist. He's seen Charlene's bare rear end, no doubt about it, and put his hands on it besides.

At times like this I wish I'd never left Barely Hollow. Everything anyone could ever want or need was right there. Family and friends, church, Company Store, even enemies if you craved some. Working the mines was hard but the money was good. And the Fun! We could always tease Cousin Tanya about getting knocked up in Fifth Grade. Cousin Matthew, of course, is a cripple, and we got lots of laughs carrying him off to the mountains and making him crawl home. Once when my little brother Billy got caught buggering a sheep Old Uncle Mose laughed so hard he fell dead right on the spot. That made everyone else laugh. Even Parson Blithe sensed God's Humor in it. At Uncle Mose's funeral the Parson said, and we're going to miss him something awful, Uncle Mose, but maybe Young Billy will take this as the Lord's Lesson not to pick out such tall sheep and look like a gol-durn fool hiking up on his tippy-toes. It might also save some lives. He said this last with a twinkle in his eye. Nobody blamed Billy for poor Uncle Mose's misery.

But it's too late now. I set my buckets of sodium carbonate in the corner for my replacement to use and slink down to Offal. I guess it won't be so bad after getting used to the smell.

The Offal Department manufactures the food that's fed to trout being raised for sale. After the trout are cleaned and packaged the heads and guts are recycled to make Trout Pellets, which are then fed to more trout being raised for sale. Disgusting? The trout don't care. They *like* Trout Pellets.

So here I am being trained by an Offalman Second Class on operation of the Conveyor and the gigantic Grinder that grinds up the heads and guts, not to mention dry meal and vitamins and minerals and other stuff added to the mix by a Hatcheryman First Class. Of course, only an Offalman First Class is qualified to run the Pelletizer, a big filthy machine that extrudes pellets like wet worms while a knife cuts them into bite-sized pieces.

It's pretty awesome standing here on the catwalk and watching trout heads and guts coming up on the Conveyor and being dumped into the Grinder and then emerging someplace else as Trout Pellets.

I'm thinking maybe if I get Charlene interested enough in the Mechanics of Offalology she won't move out.

My first assignment is to stand underneath the Conveyor and pick up any heads and guts that fall off. As you might imagine, this job is lowest of the low in terms of status and filth. I make sure to wear my hat, the one that says Chew Mail Pouch—Treat Yourself to the Best. It helps some, but I still cringe when a trout head bounces off the bill. When guts are falling I can hear a sort of splat! and know something's sticking to me someplace. Then it's Hide-And-Seek with trout guts doing the hiding and me the seeking. After a couple of hours I'm relieved by another Offalman Third Class, a kid just out of school. He doesn't have any teeth and when the first head bounces off his hatless skull he laughs real high-pitched and says, ish thish wild or what?

During Break I lean against the Grinder drinking a Diet Dr Pepper and hobnobbing with the other Offalmen. They're not a bad bunch. I don't notice any particular odor because we all smell the same. They ask me what things are like up topside at Hatchery. I think it's sad that nobody in Offal considers himself part of the Big Picture. To them it's Hatchery and Offal. They see themselves as just Offalmen doing an Offalman's job: heads and guts, guts and heads, occasionally a sack of meal or a gallon jug of vitamin. One old guy winks and says, yep, one time I drunk me a whole jug of them vitamins. I'll tell you, boys, my Missus was plenty sore down there Between the Legs! Everyone laughs. This is Offalman Talk. We think of ourselves as a Pretty Tough Bunch. We take it on the chin and give it right back. Morale isn't so bad as you might suspect.

We're about ready to return to our jobs when Mr. Owensworth breezes in. Alright you Disgusting Turds, he says. Listen up because I'm not saying this twice. The stench is awful! How can you people put up with conditions down here in Offal? Anyhow, take a short break to participate in this Employee Betterment Hologram. Form a circle and hold hands. That's right. My, aren't we cute! A bunch of Stinking Offalmen holding hands. Good Jesus Christ. Okay, here goes.

Mr. Owensworth clicks on the module, and suddenly we're part of a holographic Presentation starring Mr. Owensworth. Except that is isn't Mr. Owensworth. He's no longer fat and dumpy with several chins. A Computer Artist has taken his basic features and skin tones and carved off about a hundred pounds of blubber. His cheeks are firm and rosy and sucked in. The arms sticking out of his Arnold Palmer golf shirt are bare and muscular. He has a full head of hair. As he turns to speak, a hank falls over his forehead. He brushes it back without a thought. Hair? Why, of course, I've always had it you know. His torso is taut and trim, his carriage straight and tall. In his left he's holding a Putter.

A smiling Mr. Owensworth admonishes us to try harder for the sake of Hatchery and God. For Ourselves, for Family, for Mr. Owensworth Himself. Most especially for the Shareholders. There is Honor in a Hard Day's Work, he tells us. Pick up those and guts and throw them joyously back onto the Conveyor! Love Your Hatchery Family and Your Hatchery Family Will Love You Back!

I break away silently, linking the hands of the Offalmen on each side of me. They seem not to notice. This is my opportunity to ask Mr. Owensworth's forgiveness and maybe get my old job back. I see him heading toward the Grinder. He walks up the steps to the catwalk, and I follow. The noise is deafening.

Mr. Owensworth pauses at the top and looks down into the roiling mass of brown meal and red offal being ground to mush. I come up behind him and tap him lightly on the shoulder. Mr. Owensworth makes a startled turn toward me and loses his balance. For an instant he teeters on the catwalk. He holds out his hand, but I can only look at it. The hand is fat and hairless, not at all like the hand of the Handsome Guy Holding The Putter. He opens his mouth and screams, but it's a silent scream; there's too much noise in Offal to hear him. Then he topples backward, landing near the edge of the vortex. I lean over for a better look thinking that Mr. Owensworth could have made a nifty cannonball if only he'd grabbed his knees. He surfaces once and disappears. There's a crunching sound audible above the background noise, loud and brief, then business as usual. I look behind me. Everyone is still watching the holographic Mr. Owensworth.

116

At the end of the presentation we go back to work. I don't say anything and nobody asks what happened to the Boss. After all, why would he have stuck around to watch his own hologram, especially in the Offal Department? All this was yesterday.

Last night Charlene says, yuck, what the hell happened to you? Where's my valise, I'm moving out. Nobody could put up with this stink. I ask her to wait until I can shower, that I have some news. Charlene likes gossip better than anything except a new tattoo, so she waits. Look, I say after showering off, stick around. Things are going to get better, maybe even between you and Ms. Swisher. I tell her about events at work and swear her to secrecy. I'll soon be back topside at Hatchery, I tell her. Not to worry, that I see pH Control once again in my future.

Sure enough, this morning I'm put back in my old job by Interim Management. Home Office suspects Mr. Owensworth of running off with some Bimbo from Marketing, although Marlene (formerly Ms. Swisher) has it on good authority that the Bimbo in question took off with her Therapist.

Tonight I come home smelling normal again, like sodium carbonate. Some of the trout are constipated. Rumor has Nutrition blaming foreign particles in yesterday's batch of Trout Pellets. Another rumor has Laboratory identifying said particles as bits of polyester from a '70s Leisure Suit. Charlene and Marlene have been to the Mall for tattoos and tongue rings. All is friendly between them. Charlene drops her 501 Levi's to show me her latest. I can't believe what a sensitive statement she's made. Starting at the top of the butt cleavage and extending downward is a full blueprint of our Conveyor-Grinder-Pelletizer Assembly over at Hatchery with all features drawn to scale in different colored inks. She spreads her cheeks and shows me where the pellets are extruded. I love you, I say. Ditto, she answers. Marlene says it's wonderful seeing us so happy.

Fat Dreams

He was fat with porcine eyes recessed within plump cheeks. Through them he saw everything and everyone, but those few who troubled to look back—if ever anyone had—saw only their reflections in the dark pupils limned against a pale blue background. Like one-way glass the view from outside revealed nothing within.

He stood anonymously with coat collar turned up against the wind, waiting patiently while a snow plow scraped past. Afterward he waited for the traffic light to change before crossing, stepping carefully over parapets of brown slush thrown up by the plow. Other pedestrians hurried past—an old woman shuffling along the slick pavement, two adolescent boys with laughing faces, an office girl with a red scarf drawn tightly across her mouth. He saw them all, but none saw him.

He walked slowly, eyes straight ahead, arriving eventually at a pastry shop. Before entering he looked right and then left, uneasily it seemed. At the counter he quickly ordered a dozen donuts. The counterman filled his request without speaking and handed back the change.

Outside again, he stood on the sidewalk and ate two donuts, then shoved the sack containing the rest into his overcoat pocket. A deep gnawing inside, more primitive than hunger, was stilled momentarily. Thoughts of "Funes the Memorious," a Borges story he had read that morning, subverted the street's reality. Blood suddenly fulminated in his ears and temples, and he felt euphoric. Dream images of astonishing dissimilitude exploded before him. The faces of pedestrians became eyeless thermograms of red, orange, and yellow; multi-colored coats, previously monochromatic in the failed light, jiggled like fire, every hue and shade distinguished by its odor and degree of warmth. By standing absolutely still he could see the intricate patterns of snowflakes grown to the size of doilies. They revolved and shimmered like iridescent frescoes, neither falling nor rising.

Finally he looked away, erasing this glittering universe by force of will and bringing back the drab one. Snow was falling heavily; late afternoon had descended into night. He continued on, passing through the main shopping district to the outskirts of town where the few shops were closed and dark. He was the only pedestrian about; the murmur of distant traffic alternately encroached and receded in the swirling wind.

He came at last to the only shop still open. Its outside lamp was dim, the sign over the door faded to obsolescence. A bell announced his entrance. He stamped off the snow and scanned the eclectic array of items. Although he had been in the shop many times the proprietress did not recognize him. There was nothing he needed or wanted; he wished merely to examine the different items, to observe their shapes, to feel their weights and textures. He appreciated the cold smoothness of antique brass and how the pages of old books were dry and dusty as moth wings.

He was preparing to leave when his gaze was diverted to a brief glow of room light reflected from a small hand mirror. He picked up the mirror and examined it, noticing that it was very old and double-sided with a gilt handle and frame. The eroded silvering reflected a dark, incomplete mosaic of his face. The mirror was strangely appealing, and he bought it. The proprietress accepted his money wordlessly. Her pale hands moved with the swift efficiency of ermines.

He returned through the snow to his small apartment in the main part of town. There, in a building he owned, above a used bookstore of which he was the proprietor, were three small rooms fronted by dirty windows. He left his shoes just inside the door and hung the topcoat on a hook. The donuts he placed in the refrigerator, the mirror on a coffee table littered with magazines.

That afternoon at the store, after returning from a large lunch, he had immersed himself in Bates' *A Naturalist on the Rivers Amazon*. He had lifted his eyes from the page and dreamed of a rainforest where he saw himself wading in a brown river. He heard the current snatching at the bank and felt mud beneath his bare feet. Other images appeared, suffused with bird calls, insect noises, the odor of rotting vegetation. The air became damp and oppressive. Rain tumbled down through the forest canopy, and on his open palm he saw a spattering of raindrops. He awoke elated and perspiring heavily, his hair and the bottoms of his trouser legs sopping wet.

He picked up the mirror absently, noticing for the first time an inscription in Latin embossed on the handle. It read *Hic quails es* (*This is how you are*), and he saw the fractured reflection of his face. Upon turning the mirror over he noticed another inscription, this one reading *Hic quails vis* (*This is how you want to be*), and saw reflected back the thin, incomplete face of a stranger. He was startled, thinking it might be a dream, but on looking again saw that the image was immediate, moving when he moved, blinking when he blinked. There could be no mistaking the reflection's identity.

He had lived alone all his adult life, nameless except to his creditors and invisible to everyone, possessed of a flat, featureless personality ill-suited to the harlequinade of daily interaction. In the absence of friends and without prospects of friendship, he had never thought about being thin and attractive, of having a lover, of socializing. These possibilities existed in lofty remoteness exceeding even the reach of his reveries, and his mind now fingered them as tentatively as if they were flowers in a strange and vibrant garden.

For no understandable reason he emptied the refrigerator and pantry, throwing all the food into large garbage bags and carrying them to the alley outside. Upon returning to his rooms he once again picked up the mirror and examined the two images. They had not changed. He then tidied up, making several more trips to the alley with stacks of magazines and newspapers. He stripped to his underclothes and vacuumed the floors; sweating furiously he scoured the bathtub, sink, and toilet until the porcelain gleamed. Finally, unaccustomed to physical exertion, he relinquished himself to the bed and fell immediately to sleep.

The next morning he awoke without the usual gnawing of hunger. Remembering the mirror he examined his images and saw with relief that everything was the same. The thin face seemed less distant now, the eyes nearly his own.

At the bookstore he fidgeted, overcome by restlessness that drove his legs to twitch and his fingers to doodle on the backs of sales slips. Within the books, previously a respite from daily tedium, slumbered the spores of claustrophobia. As for the bookshelves, metamorphosis into prison bars had been instantaneous and complete, their narrowing lines seeming to preclude any escape. For the first time he was grateful when a customer appeared; for nearly the first time he attempted conversation.

Having been disrupted briefly, his pattern in the ensuing weeks became fixed once more: upon awakening, a glance at his images in the mirror, now taken almost for granted; he showered, shaved, and dressed, leaving the apartment without breakfast. Then came dull days at the store with every minute of the boredom lived fully: untidy snow seen through a streaked window, pedestrians wandering without evident purpose like inhabitants of a stockyard, the day's grayness slipping interminably toward black. Lunches were coffee and salad in a cafeteria where he became a voyeur of the feeding process, observing with practiced discretion those mechanisms by which food is transferred to the mouth, chewed, and swallowed. Dinner at the same table was followed by evenings walking the dark streets before returning to straighten up the apartment, undress, sleep.

As time passed the frequency and intensity of his dreams attenuated—first to abbreviated images without beauty or scent, then to just sounds, then nothing. It was as if his senses had been misplaced temporarily and he had only to search for them in the right places. The possibility that the capacity to dream had been lost did not alarm him. He had always considered his reveries to be outgrowths of eating and reading, but food and books were no longer interesting.

The snow finally melted, leaving behind occasional crusts huddling in dark crevices like fragments of memory; then one day they too were gone. Birds returned, and for the first time he watched them. The lengthening daylight extended into the dim yards to the white houses, their door frames parted like lips, peeling and chapped, softened by the gloss of azaleas. Sunsets exploded abruptly behind lavender hills, trees faded to silhouettes at dusk. Every image became an impoverished apparition of the previous unreality, now slipping away as if through someone else's fingers.

At night he and his new acquaintances descended like noisy starlings onto the metal chairs of an outdoor café. He was thin and fashionably dressed, large-eyed now. His old clothes had been discarded gradually, stuffed into garbage bags and abandoned in the alley. Periodically he took a bus to a neighboring city and purchased replacements. The clerks there knew him by name and greeted him with smiles.

She was one of the café group. All that spring she had watched him, absorbing reflections from his renewed image and imprinting them onto her own until the graft became comfortable. Soon conversation, like the daylight, lengthened and gained warmth, forcing aside all irrelevancies. They stopped listening to other voices and other sounds except their own. Her perfume drew him like a pheromone; details of her skin became a familiar landscape, and he heard in her breasts a rhythmic sighing like the synchronous breathing of sleeping cats. She took his hand while they talked and placed it on her knee, gauging without expression its electric effect, reconstructing in her own mind his mental image of smooth skin underneath the coolness of nylon.

One night she took him home to her white house that floated, it seemed, on a dark lawn, her image of him now larger and more complex than the one he reflected. She went into the bedroom, undressed, and stood naked before him in the doorway. He sat silently, surprised at her hair glistening with halos, breasts pale and pink-rimmed, legs long and muscular and vaguely frightening. They made love. He could not see her eyes, but he remembered the white hands now stepping lightly over his skin, cunning and quick as ermines.

In summer they hiked among the hills, emerging from shadows onto pinnacles that stood bunched and upright against slanted afternoons. Once they came to a stream, its water alternately flowing like Hippocrene through still pools and over stones, insidious, and he thought he heard overhead the wing beats of a horse. They picnicked there, made love among the ferns, fell asleep. He awoke at dusk while she still slept. In the dappled light her breasts and waist and the long curves of her legs were patterned with moving stripes, and he saw her as a great beast propelled by subterranean engines. He was suddenly afraid that she would feed on him until nothing remained except gnawed bones.

Few remnants of his previous life remained by autumn. His clothes had been packed and moved to the white house where they hung in uneasy juxtaposition with hers or lay folded in unfamiliar drawers. The windows of his apartment were closed and locked and the curtains drawn as if to incarcerate and punish the sad contents left behind. His bookstore had been abandoned too, although the inventory remained to be sold. Days were spent at the antique shop where she instructed him in nuances of the business and supervised the few minor repair jobs that his awkwardness permitted him to perform.

At night they frequented an indoor café, no longer talking intimately but participating in the larger conversations. His role was that of observer, seldom speaking unless addressed, sensing in her animated replies and interjections—and confirmed by the eyes of the listeners—a degree of participation adequate for them both. His mind drifted, hearing in the disjointed weave of phrases a verbal fabric as comfortless as ratiné. His views were seldom sought, and he declined to offer any.

It had been so easy, these games played to hesitant conclusions. He recognized among myriad rituals of café life certain elements used in his approbation and final acceptance: silence misinterpreted as interest, a few words offered in conversation mistaken for wisdom. And her? She had been a lamp, he a newly hatched chrysalis.

Knowing this, she had offered the narrow orbit of herself in exchange for his unrestricted range of the dark.

One winter evening he stood and left the café. Suddenly he missed his former life and its refuge of dreaming. In that relict existence there was room only for one. He pulled up the collar of his coat and walked through the empty streets to the bookstore. Cobwebs hung from the shelves, and the floor was littered with mouse droppings. He sat in his chair among the dusty books feeling at ease for the first time in months. He chose several volumes and went upstairs.

The apartment was also dusty and unkempt, although tolerable. He took off his coat and turned up the heat. Soon the rooms were warm, and he read most of Piccard and Dietz's *Seven Miles Down* before finally closing the book and setting it aside. Piccard's adventure had been, in his own words, the *grande plongée*.

Without warning a dream appeared, tepid and fragmented—a ghost of his former dreams, but a dream nonetheless. In it he was one of two crew members aboard the bathyscaphe *Trieste* descending onto the blue depth of the Pacific. At a thousand feet the lights had been switched on, and he saw before him in the forward beam an endless blizzard of plankton appearing to fall upward, heightening the illusion of speed as *Trieste* plummeted like an elevator toward the Mariana Trench, the deepest place on Earth. The thought that the ship might be grabbed by abyssal currents and dashed against unseen canyon walls brought a flood of bile to his throat, and he fought back nausea. His feet felt cold against the steel hull chilled now by icy water outside. At twenty thousand feet they passed the depth of the abyssal plain, which stretches around the world, and plunged onward, deeper than Mt. Everest is tall. Ballast was dropped; the rate of descent slowed. He could hear only an affricative hiss of oxygen into their tiny sphere and the metallic click of instrument switches. Finally touchdown in the Challenger Deep at more than thirty-five thousand feet and a hull pressure of two hundred thousand tons. Red shrimps flitted like cardinals through their powerful beams. A flounder rose languidly from the ivory-colored ooze and swam off into blackness.

He awoke sweating. He walked to the coffee table, picked up the mirror, and looked at his reflection. In the side with the inscription that read *Hic quails es* he saw his familiar face, thin and troubled. In the reverse side he saw a nondescript fat man. He sighed with relief and checked his watch. The pastry shop might still be open, but he would have to hurry.

Batness

I WAS ROLLING A second doobie of Uncle Bill's Shredded Weed soaked in Uncle Bill's Special Hash Oil Sauce when I heard a scrabbling noise like mice make, except mice don't normally live inside chimneys. Unbalanced dichotomies of natural and unnatural origin have always held a fascination. I glanced up at this thought and adjusted its level, reminding myself not to smoke the kids' Shredded Wheat by mistake.

I looked at my watch, but the sweep hand seemed to have stopped. Either that or its speed had accelerated until I could detect elements of motion only intermittently, like glimpsing the spokes of a moving wagon wheel. Nothing serious, fortunately. Uncle Bill's products sometimes had this effect, although the brain damage was seldom permanent.

I sprinkled a heaping dollop of Uncle Bill's Shredded Weed into a creased cigarette paper, then carefully folded over the bottom edge. My fingers responded like frozen hooves. I was Bambi rolling a joint. I thought of Sam Spade rolling his own cigarettes in *The Maltese Falcon* and pouncing on Miss Wonderly, she of the thick red hair and blue, blue eyes. Ah yes! I giggled, then sneezed, then had to start over. Should have rolled two at the beginning instead of rolling just one and smoking it. Poor planning. I chuckled. I laughed out loud.

Suddenly another laugh answered mine. The laugh seemed to

come from all around, bounding off the walls and boxes, floor and windows. I looked toward the unlit fireplace. Staggering around on the hearth was a rumpled gray object. It was a chubby rat trying to unfurl an umbrella. Either that or a diminutive Rumpole of the Bailey just leaving a Lilliputian pub. Rat or Rumpole, it was covered with soot.

This is no time to panic, I thought. Stay calm. *Roll. . .the. . .doobie.* That's it. Ol' Sam had nothing on you, boy. Just pull the string with your teeth and close the pouch. Hell, pretend it's Bull Durham. Zippppp! Good work! Shee-*it*. Ain't nothing finah than the dope in Caro-lina.

The object shifted. It laughed again, right at me this time. The sound was like chalk screeching across slate. I winced reflexively. The object coughed and unfurled its umbrella halfway. I held out a palm. No raindrops. Why the umbrella? We were indoors and it wasn't raining. At least I didn't think so. Maybe it *was* raining. The *I Ching* probably could probably confirm it. Did this house have a roof? I couldn't be sure. I'd just moved in a couple of days before, and who ever looks up? All our stuff was piled around in boxes. Maybe I got ripped off. God-*damn*! Just like that snotty realtor to rent me a roofless house. And now it was raining. Easy. Relax. Ignite the end and imbibe a small toke. Pick up match. Like this (scratch, puff, puff). Ah! Much better. Deal with the roof tomorrow. Can always leave, of course, demand my deposit. That bitch. Where was the contract? Find it tomorrow and look for a clause saying "Deposit nonreturnable even if tenant notices absence of a roof." No doubt in the tiniest print. I looked up. Jesus. Nighttime. The sky was black.

The object on the hearth laughed again. I winced again. "I wish you wouldn't do that, Rumpole," I said. "Either stop or take laughing lessons."

"Rumpole? Who the hell is Rumpole?" the umbrellaed object asked.

"I thought you were," I said.

"Never heard of Rumpole," came a reply accompanied by a cough. "However, I do know something about smoking bats out of chimneys." (Cough, cough.) "I've been smoked out of three chimneys" (cough) "and a belfry myself, but never with smoke like this. What is it?"

"Uncle Bill's Shredded Weed soaked in Uncle Bill's Special Hash Oil Sauce," I said, taking a toke and blowing it at the fireplace. "Primo stuff."

"That's definitely true," Not-Rumpole answered while inhaling deeply.

I leaned forward and tried to focus. Couldn't be Ken unfurling his umbrella for Barbie. Ken never needed a shave, and where was Barbie? "If you're not Rumpole, who are you"

"I'm a bat," Not-Rumpole-the-Bat said.

I leaned back warily. "Are you rabid?"

"I don't think so," the bat replied. "On second thought, you're bigger and more dangerous. Whether I'm rabid or not will stay my little secret. Keep away from me, and don't go reaching for any brooms. Anyhow, I can't fly while under influence of smoke. Not to fear that I'll leap into the air and go flapping around your head."

"I don't own a broom," I said.

"No kidding," the bat answered sarcastically. It was turning its head this way and that and sound was bouncing every which way. Its high pitch was hurting my ears.

"Stop it!" I shouted. "I can't stand that goddamn squeaking!"

"Sorry," the bat replied. "Just getting my bearings. We bats use echolocation, you know. Christ, this place is a dump. It's dirtier than the inside of a chimney."

"Never mind my housekeeping," I said testily. "You think I've never been inside a bat cave? I know how you guys live."

"Got me there," said the bat. It started to lick itself.

"What're you doing?" I asked. "Why are you licking yourself?"

"I'm grooming. It's how we bats stay clean."

"Well, do it somewhere else. I think it's disgusting." I took another toke and blew smoke toward the hearth. The bat sniffed it in. "Say," I remarked. "This is a golden opportunity. You see, I've just finished reading Thomas Nagel's essay, 'What Is It Like to Be a Bat?' Being a bat yourself, a vespertilian opinion would count for a lot."

"What's the point?" asked the bat.

"Well, Nagel concluded that a human can never know what it's like to be another species. The question isn't what it might be like for *me* to be a bat, but what it's like for *you* actually being one. Incidentally, what's your name?"

"Name? I don't understand."

"What do other bats call you?"

"They don't."

"Oh. Then may I call you Rumpole?"

"Sure," said Rumpole. "After all, what's in a name?"

"Do you mind if I record our conversation?" I asked. "I'm an unemployed philosophy professor. My application for tenure was denied at my last post. Had to move on. Knowing the answer to Nagel's question would make—I mean *make*—my academic reputation."

"I don't mind," Rumpole said.

"Hot damn!" I opened the drawer beside me and got out the portable recorder, plugged it in, and turned the switch. Green and red lights flashed. "Okay, so what's it like to be a bat?"

"That's difficult to explain," Rumpole said, "without knowing what it's like to be *you*. Inevitably the problem of species polarity clouds our mutual understanding. For example, I don't see too well, but my echolocation capabilities allow me to scan your outline. I therefore know your general size and shape and that you're not edible. At least not to me. A vampire bat might feel differently, of course. Do you humans have echolocation?"

"Unfortunately, no," I answered, instinctively rubbing the bridge of my nose where I'd blundered into a closed door. "Vision is our principal sense, but there are exceptions. Take me, for instance. Without glasses I'm blind as a. . . well, you know."

I got up and shuffled in slow motion to the bookcase.

"What are you doing?" Rumpole asked.

"Looking for a book. Ah, here it is, Philip Roth's *Sabbath's Theater*. Indeedy yes." I thumbed the pages until finding the passage. "Listen up," I said. "Roth, talking through Sabbath, his protagonist, ponders whether mankind is the only species that awakens with a morning erection. He asks, 'Do whales? Do bats?'" I snapped the book shut and dropped it on the floor. "So do you?"

"Do I what?" asked Rumpole

"Wake up with a morning erection?"

Rumpole replied, "Don't be stupid. In the morning we're all jockeying for position so we can hang upside-down in the cave and go to sleep."

"Of course!" I cried, easing back in my chair. "So do you wake up with an *evening* erection? C'mon, you can tell me."

"It's none of your business," Rumpole said with finality.

"What's the big deal?" I asked.

"Nothing, except that your species appears to be oversexed. We bats have more important things to consider, such as where to roost once inside our cave, how to get enough to eat, stuff like that."

Not to be outdone, I replied, "We have housing and food shortages too."

"Quite so," answered Rumpole, "except in your case the species goes right on fornicating. In fact, your breeding rate seems to quicken as the availability of housing and food diminishes." He looked at me myopically and grinned. "You're a devil," he said.

"Let's get back on track," I admonished. "I believe we were discussing what it's like to be a bat."

"Pretty routine," Rumpole said. "There's lots of pushing and shoving and shrieking at each other, lots of hanging upside-down shoulder to shoulder, the odor of bat shit wafting up your nostrils day in and day out, a steady diet of bugs, sex maybe once or twice a year unless your partner has a headache."

"Sounds terrible," I said.

"Terrible? It's pretty great, actually, but then what could you know?'

"More than you think, smart guy. I used to live in New York. You want pushing and shoving and shrieking? Try crossing Eighth Avenue at rush hour. In New York lots of us stood shoulder to shoulder hanging right-side up from subway straps. We smelled the dog shit, ate bugs in our mashed potatoes at the Automat, and my Friday night date always had a headache." Rumpole shrugged his umbrella.

"Actually," I continued, "you've just told me what life is like *as a* bat, not what it's like *to be* a bat. Let's approach the question differently. What is it you do best? I mean, in all the world." This was a trick question. If Rumpole answered that flying around was what he did best or echolocation or hanging upside-down or contributing to the community guano heap, then maybe I had opened a hidden door to a lengthy corridor at the end of which resided my Holy Grail: batness, bat-hood, whatever.

Rumpole wrinkled his forehead and considered deeply before speaking. " I would have to say that being a bat is what I do best."

"That's not what I meant!" I leaned forward, the better to make my point. "For example, if I asked a human the same question the reply might be, 'I'm best at motherhood' or 'I run the mile best' or 'I work an abacus best.' Get the idea?" I sat back and awaited Rumpole's reply.

"It's the same thing," said Rumpole. "Those answers describe various human activities, not states of being. They're not even understandable unless the interrogator already has some notion about them—a mental image, so to speak. Even then they don't tell you what it's like *to be* a human. You might as well ask another human what it's like to be a bat."

"You're right," I told him. For some reason I wasn't thinking clearly. "Then would it be fair to say that bats are solipsists?"

"It wouldn't be too far wrong," Rumpole replied, "considering I'm unable to verify anyone's consciousness except my own. Naturally, I can't speak for other bats without knowing what it's like being them." He then added hastily, "assuming other bats are conscious, of course." He grinned slyly. The inside of his mouth looked like a pincushion. "Are you conscious?"

I said, "You're a pain in the ass. This conversation is exasperating."

"Rumpole said, "Careful. I haven't mentioned what kind of bat I am. Maybe I really am a vampire bat. Maybe I'll take a bite out of your ass and give you a real pain."

"I'd stomp you flat." I felt menacing.

"My, my, aren't we getting nasty. Typical of your species. Kill this, slaughter that, eradicate this or that. Smoke out bats in the name of public health."

"Well, your sort does carry rabies," I said.

"True enough," Rumpole replied. "And yours doesn't carry syphilis and gonorrhea and leprosy?"

"Okay," I said. "Truce. Let's return to the subject. What's it like to be a bat. For example, how do you distinguish your own kind of bat from other kinds?"

"What a stupid question. Obviously we insectivores are superior. Fishing bats eat raw fish, which is pretty disgusting (imagine their breath). Vampire bats eat blood, which is even more disgusting. And picture living in the same cave with fifty thousand fruit bats, all of them with diarrhea."

"Ah, so bats disapprove of miscegenation. That's very interesting. It affirms a speciesist viewpoint. We humans, of course, are a single species, and 'speciesist'—stupid term though it is—can't apply to us."

"It doesn't?" Rumpole was incredulous. "Bugshit! Remember, it's not uncommon for one of your races to smoke out bats and then blame their presence on another race's inferior hygiene. Ha! Don't try convincing me it isn't human races pitted against each other and all of you against all of us. Call it what you like, but it's still xenophobia."

I ignored this outburst, forgetting what I was about to say. Another toke recharged the memory banks. "Face it, Your Batness, if we humans have smoked out one bat we've smoked out the lot of you. All bats look alike to us," I said.

"Hardly an original observation," was Rumpole's caustic reply. "As I've explained, any bat can easily distinguish a bat of another species. However, I can accept a one-species hypothesis where humans are concerned. According to our echolocation scans your tissue densities and general outlines seldom vary. Any distinctions are caused by the clothes. Butt naked, all humans reflect sound alike to us bats."

Somehow I rolled another doobie. The effort was heroic. Our intense conversation continued along these lines, give and take, another. . . how long? I must have fallen asleep because Monica was shaking me.

"What's going on?" she said.

"Must have been sleeping," I said, rubbing my eyes.

"What the hell is this? I send you ahead with the moving van three days ago. I quit a good job in Philly when you have only the prospect of another lousy gig here in North Carolina. And what happens? Nothing is unpacked, and you're stoned!" She folded her arms and glared down at me. "The kids are outside."

"Yes, but great news. I've managed to address Nagel's question about. . ."

Monica interrupted. "What's that smell? Were you cooking?"

Suddenly I remembered. "I fried up some insects. Green-bottle flies, a few crickets, and maybe a cockroach. Oh, and a moth."

Monica sat down on the arm of my chair. "What's on your lip?" She peeled away the object and held it up. I examined it closely.

"Fly wing," I said.

"That's disgusting. You come down here and sit around smoking dope and eating bugs. I should have listened to my parents. They told me you were terminally weird." She set her purse on the floor.

"I was trying to understand what it's like to be a bat, but never mind. Wait till you hear this. It's going to change everything. Nagel's views were correct, and I now have the first direct evidence that no species can ever know what it's like to be another. I got it by interviewing a bat." I turned to the recorder and pushed the Play button. Nothing happened. I turned up the volume. Still nothing.

Monica glanced at the recorder. "There's no cassette in it," she muttered. "You really are a moron when it comes to anything mechanical."

I slumped down in the chair. It was over. So much for a future tenure-track position.

"What's that?" Monica got up from the chair arm and walked over to the hearth. "Ugh. It's a dead bat. How did it get in here? Does this place have bats?"

"It fell down the chimney last night. Its name is Rumpole. We were debating Nagel's question about the essence of batness."

"Then you debated it with yourself. This bat's a mummy. It's been dead about a hundred years."

"Aw, bugshit," I said softly.

"Say again?"

"Nothing."

Blue Unicorn

His face was a mudslide, steel-wool hair sudsed white in the sea mist. *But the Lord provided a great fish to swallow Jonah, and Jonah was inside the fish three days and three nights*, I quoted and heard the echo.

He looked my way, I thought, but the light and he were both dark. *And the Lord commanded the fish, and it vomited Jonah onto dry land*, I went on, flopping in the surf like a beached porpoise. Then I puked for the second or more probably continuous time, watching neon pulses of discrete indigestibles flood the sparkling sand.

Her thoughts were a fish's: I held them; they were nothing. No great flight of alienness, just silence in place of the mewling noises that people make, jaws working silently up and down to pump water in, pump water out, sensuous lips more firm than cartilage and sucking around like bellows.

She's a fish, I announced. He didn't reply, believing me to be crazy or worse. However, I'm safe now, I continued. You can rest easy, I got well away.

Do you partake, my friend? I asked him. Are you a tonguer of Tabs, an imbiber of Blotter? Do you blow the Blue Unicorn, whisper Wedding Bells, sashay in the Sunshine, have a Ticket to Ride? In short, do you deposit LSD into the closed system of yourself?

He looked my way casual as hell. No man, I'm a drunk.

Aha! Now we arrive at, as it were the crux of the matter, the nexus, so to speak, the secret moist locus where something finally is sacred that's not surrounded by hair. A thing dark is right here among us lurking *and it is not nooky*, which in this desperate light resembles a small hummock in an unshaven swamp. Maybe sawgrass or cattails. Do you follow, fellow eremite?

I'm just your standard drunk and we don't see much, even looking down at our feet.

I see *her*, or rather, I did.

Who, man?

Lucy in the Sky with Diamonds.

Them are stars, cousin, it's night. I see his head crank back like the pan of a tripod. I picture his eyes as dual telescopes dialing in the planets, dropping tears on their moons.

Moon their eyes, I say. I see her, I say. She's getting pumped by Bart Simpson plain as day, Lucy is, plain as your face, which isn't exactly because of the flowing of collagen downhill following that erosion map, the sharp inversion of the nose (nostrils pointed straight up), eyebrows in a plate tectonic shift. Looky there, behind us! See the brightness!

That ain't the sky, cousin, it's the casinos over Biloxi way lit up like Christmas. Folks are bleeding money, they surely are. He tipped back his head again and this time poured whiskey into an opening that was above the horizon but still invisible. The opening made smacking sounds, could be wet.

My god! She looked like a human woman, although she was not a woman, my lord no, she was a fish, some sort of bass, I think, maybe a perch, a perciform fish. Her eyes were a permanent stare situation, irises like a fixed residency.

I'm requesting a neural transplant, I continued in a voice full of thoughts doubtfully obtuse. Sever the ganglia and substitute chips of silicon. (I waved my arms as a circuits check.) Extract the few brain cells left undamaged, detox in Thorazine, and grow on top of chips in a Petri dish. Implant chips in skull, insert bone lid like manhole cover and suture flaps of skin, fire neurons. If I shit instead of uttering vowels, some random adjustment directed by control knobs sticking of my skull should do the trick. The docs and techs ought to have lots of laughs. Hey Harriett, want to see him piss and roll his eyes? Give that knob—yeah, that one—a quarter-turn to the left, yeah, that's right, good. Not too far or he'll anally crepitate all over your designer lab coat.

My premorbid adjustments are paltry notwithstanding, accounting for the recent bad trip. The soul is light and spongy as a crêpe, to which aforementioned bumpy ride attests. I can lie down on mine and roll up in it like it's a dirty blanket. Want to see? Watch.

Say, fool, don't be rolling around in that wet sand. I catch your drift. Bad acid trip. Flashbacks.

Flashbacks my ass! These visions are real. I *know* my mermaid, old son, how she was conceived outside the body in cold seawater in an unlit open womb of mud and plankton. She wanted my sperm discharged around her in a cloud, she sought to wallow in sperm. External fertilization is all the rage out there down under, eggs and sperm everywhere, in your mouth, ears, gills. When we held hands her palm was slippery with ctenoid scales. Trust me, those Sirens don't sing to anyone unless they're another species semi-aquatic enough to climb out onto the rocks and reefs. Prufrock heard only the ringing in his ears. Ask yourself whether God stops breezes or brakes wind.

Now I can wonder, art thou a leg man? Interesting how a woman only five feet tall can't have truly great legs but one a mere six inches longer can dent hearts with hers, leave on a man's mind a lecherous image of the slinky form. Six inches make all the difference. I say the world turns on six inches, the length of my personal penis going unstated and unmeasured in present masculine company. Rest relaxed. I'm not one of *them*, no pecker-waving from this collapsing window.

I'm a T and A man myself, he answers, or used to be. I went for a goodly set and wideness of butt. Nothing wasted, that's my motto. Got me in a dash of trouble too, heh, heh. Still standing, he takes a swallow the bottle.

You coming out of it, cousin? he asks. You was rolling around in the low surf sucking on a big dead fish when I first come on you.

Somebody had caught him way out in the Gulf and cut off his filets, and the remains washed ashore here on this beach. What you
snuggled up beside of was a Sylvester-the-Cat kind of a fish, all head
and backbone and ribs, no meat left. Man, your mouth was pressed
against them cold wet lips and giving full tongue, and your thumb
was stuck in a hole where the heart must of been at one time, when
that fish was alive and swimming on its way somewheres, and you
was muttering about what a icy bitch she was, and I asked who, and
you said this goddamn mermaid without a beating heart.

Sleep's impossible. I have insomnia. Either that or the scrofula.
Give me a drink.

I'm just a old sot, and I need this for medical reasons. I ain't got
any money. You got money for a new bottle?

Sure, but it's wet. Here. I reached into my pocket and handed
over a wad of dripping bills. Keep it all. Buy us a bottle of mao-tai, at
the very least cheap bourbon. His eyes brightened and his mudslide
lifted in defiance of gravity, him staggering with the bottle an open
cudgel and wiping off its mouth with a filthy sleeve in deference to
me, a man of obvious taste and a connoisseur of cryptarithms.

At dawn and dusk we rose out of the dank sticky ooze to feed on
tiny fishes, anchovies probably. I couldn't bear the taste and mixed
mine (still wriggling) with a little seaweed. Horrible. I appreciate
antipasto as much as the next guy, but I like it to be dead. She would
look at me through the gloom with her own dead eyes, never smiling, distracted by what I mistook for lust and expressed by rubbing
against large amberjacks that tilted sideways reflecting silver.

Oh, no loyalty here! My mermaid was a group-spawner devoid
of personal attachments, her blood the temperature of the sea, torso slippery, tail forked and barely sexy. Titties, you ask? To tell the
truth I can scarcely remember them, like sucking on scaled sushi.
Not hair as we know hair, but more akin to the barbels of a catfish, trailing and fleshy and sticking out at all angles waving in the
eddies. Hydra woman incarnate but without the guile. She never
could have come ashore or the stuff would mat and collapse into
mucus. No perms at thirty fathoms.

Conversation? Unexperienced and unknown, certainly. She grunted on the rare occasion, similar to a species of drum mind you, an unblackened redfish. And I was, like, supposed to *understand* this. She only really grunted loudly when she wanted some sperm. Even then I had to, you know, do it myself by hand because I didn't want those cold slimy fins touching it after the first few times.

Penetration was out, you realize, as with most fish species, and participants get their jollies by administering a good fuck to the whole ocean and hoping a member of the opposite sex is close enough to be appreciative. Yessir, in ocean fucking propinquity and current direction are everything, X marks the spot, but at least you can't miss it.

Here, he said, take your ownself a teensie sip, and he gave it up.

Thank you, I accept. Ah! The sweet restfulness of the dipsomaniac. Shorten your stature beside me on the beach.

That sumbitch is wet. Me, I'll stand.

Acid parachutes your mind down onto very small and peculiar details, namely, in this instance, elemental components of the tidal wrack. With booze it's the other way around and everyone tries to solve no less peculiar problems such as world hunger, the AIDS epidemic, and how to keep the Christian Coalition off the Internet. Spaken thusly, hand over the bottle again so I can broaden my view. I'm bored with addressing sand gnats in an oratory voice, but that's hours in the past, maybe days ago, who knows. Either I was barfed up onto this beach by a quite large Jonahfish or the sand gnats were already in my mouth from kissing a decaying carcass and got barfed up instead. I saw them dragging their tiny wings through it, mine or someone else's, one of *her* relatives.

Are you from around these parts?

Which parts? This can't be Amurrica 'cause we're talking English here.

Gulfport, Mississippi, cousin.

I felt a silent spell creep near enough to grip hard. Flashback retroflexion soon to be garrulous again, enough time gathered within. Thoughts tend to digress and refract outward as the swimming mind nears the surface. I could scent loblollies from the piney woods beyond, hear angels squawk. Mineola's face bobbing from deep black water portended no fishy scales, was without slime except for a thin layer of diatoms such as encrust dead eyelids.

I drank only Laphroaig malt whisky in those days, wore a Rolex watch and deck shoes made of breast leather from a peafowl. Assuming the perverse foppery of yachters we stepped aboard our Shearwater 46 (stocked thoughtfully beforehand by servants) for a weekend cruise out to blue water, memory cupboards full of marlin skies and waves worn white on indigo. There was never any doubt, the wealth stacked cleanly atop fried catfish and hushpuppy franchises all over the Deep South. Cat-and-pup magnate, that was us, or rather, me.

First Mate Lardly Towers greeted us at the dock with salutes and the tanned helping hand aboard, after which he hummed relentlessly in falsetto much to the annoyance of our grim Ahab Cap'n Dip Thong, late of Ho Chi Minh City by way of Bakersfield and Shreveport. A merry crew made merrier by well-stocked larders of pharmaceuticals and alcoholic toxicants to which everyone had a key. (Guests and Crew, attention! The bong is now lit continuously!)

Mineola, the Lord bless her, shucked sandals on the aft deck and sat pensively sucking her left big toe (the one in ten lacking nail polish), foot anchored by breast shadows, and uttering labroidental musings from around her lip corners. At such times it was best to not speak harshly. I slunk away and made the rounds. We were self-contained for extended periods: cabin fully *en suite*, the forward heads fronted by our cozy saloon with hideaway chart table, shipshape storage for fireworks, engine box hinged with gas strut for easy access, the butterfly skylight and exquisite joinery. . . I could go on. Beware all fishes!

My fetching Mineola had been named by her father after a town in New York State and cursed a lifetime, through no fault of hers, by strangers mispronouncing it Minneapolis, even Minnehaha. To call her either was a piss-off best avoided.

I signalled to cast lines ashore. Lardly hopped to, unmuzzling the mizzen (or whatever sailors do), and we were soon astride the bounding main bucked this and that way by a devilish storm. We let the baited hand lines trail over the stern while Lardly stoked our mainsail, tweaked the jib, and Cap'n Dip Thong hove into such a wild reach that the sea thundered in fractured cataracts across the decks. Buoyed by immoderate quantities of Mind Detergent dampened with alcohol I rolled with my fighting chair as the waves changed colors, head tipped back in the blissful rain, stabbing my tongue at the sea-ends of lightning bolts as might any cosmic sword-swallower.

Mineola—adequate if not spectacular in longness of the leg—was leaning over the rail of the pitching deck huffing greatly as she pulled in a line, butt cleavage pointed optimistically at the tattooed back, biceps bulging with the strain, when suddenly she flipped overboard.

Min! I shouted, trying desperately to untab a can of beer. But the sea overcame both shouts and grief: no matter how many cans I opened the first swallow had a salty taint. Only afterward did I learn that the captain had mistakenly put us on a northeasterly course. Ten days later we discovered ourselves becalmed in the Sargasso Sea, sails flapping like wings of a moribund gull, stores depleted. Under a sobering sun I announced Min's fate. My crew had not noticed her absence but voted to mourn nonetheless.

Interrupted reverie. . . .Did you come across any golden cities? he asks.

Golden cities? Mind moths accompanied by the dry heaves broke free and fluttered aimlessly.

Under the sea. With that mermaid bitch.

Ah, you mean cities of merfolk. The mythical cities of coral and pearl where a tail-flip sends you drifting along shaded avenues lined with giant kelp and the view through everyone's picture window is an aquarium scene. Sidewalks paved with gold and silver bullion from ancient shipwrecks, no hotdog stands, just seafood wherever you turn. King Neptune runs a clam stand there.

I reckon so, yeah. I read somewhere that mermaids live in cities at the bottom of the sea. Is it true?

Naw, the closest thing I saw was an oyster-shell bank in Mobile

Bay. Very dingy, more like a tenement. The place hadn't ever been dusted, and when you kicked your feet the shit-brown silt came billowing up at your face. The view also truly sucked.

So you don't believe in them?

I didn't say that. I only said I never actually saw one. Maybe my little mermaid tootsie was an amberjack groupie, a seagoing Dead-head. Maybe her karma was following migrating fishes around hop-ing one might notice her and divulge a sperm cloud.

Hey, cousin, I don't need all this bread. Take it back except for a couple of twenties. I'm headed over to that Junior Food Mart across the street for a sixer of cold Buds and maybe cigarettes and snacks. Men got to eat. You stay here and get warm. Sun coming up. I'll get us a bottle of good sipping whiskey too, but have to look around for that.

He recaptured both his mudslide and his hair and left.

I lay back in the wet sand. What I needed was a handful of morn-ing glory seeds washed down with single-malt scotch, maybe ac-companied by a thai-stick. Somewhere palm fronds crackled and a gambler aboard a riverboat stuck squatly in the Mississippi mud gunned down his atavistic companion who had insisted loudly that if riverboats can't float they at least ought to try. The assailant wore a sweatshirt that said Motherfucker, but there could have been two words or one hyphenated. I considered this effect to be merely hal-lucinatory, not containing baroque overtones of any consequence, and searched my pockets for a bottle of dry Valium.

Creatures similar to angels or bats were in the air, disguised as crows. I noticed finally and accepted my personal layer of encrusted diatoms as evidence of prolonged immersion, exhuming memories of the glinting tapetum, the sprightly filets. . . Were you really? Her?

Partly Sunny (Or Cloudy)

I SAY IT'S PARTLY cloudy outside, she says partly sunny. I say what's the difference, she says attitude. What do sun and clouds have to do with attitude, I wonder out loud. Everything, she replies, eavesdropping on my thoughts. By saying partly cloudy I'm unconsciously telegraphing a basic pessimistic outlook, she explains. That is, assuming something as vague as a person's "outlook" could be classified as anything, including pessimistic, I reply.

We're walking down the street on a nice spring day. The sky has withheld clouds, which relegates our discussion to the abstract. Listen, she says, I hear bells chiming. We stop to listen and about fifty little kids clatter past us holding sheets of colored construction paper above their heads. They're shrieking like banshees. They remind me of leaf-cutter ants running mindlessly along the jungle floor helter-skelter, each with a piece of a leaf over its head. But ants, of course, don't scream, at least not so a person could hear it. Balloons are everywhere because today is a holiday.

I hear bells *ringing*, I say, partly for the response. Pavlov's dog had nothing on her. In his case it was a dinner bell that started him slavering.

You see what I mean? she says, her eyes narrowing. I say chime and you correct me and say ring. It really pisses me off. And now that we're on the subject, she continues, I want to put last night's discussion to rest once and for all. (Translation: I want to continue last night's discussion until death parts us one from the other and we meet in Hell, Heaven, or Wherever and pick up its loathsome trail once again.)

Okay, I reply. (What choice do I have?) Today is a beautiful day. Birds are singing, bells are chiming (or ringing), children are laughing and yelling and behaving in the simian ways of children. Pedestrians are jostling each other in the not-so-friendly way of pedestrians for whom it's just another day at the office—holiday or not, clouds or no clouds, bells or no bells.

Let's start at the beginning when you snapped at me, she says. She squeezes the fingers of one hand together and makes a mouth using her thumb as the lower jaw. Snapper, she says, opening and closing her hand-made mouth. Snapper, I repeat. Good, she says. We're on the same page. This is progress. You admit you snapped. I admit it, I admit.

Why did you snap? Wait! I'll answer that. Because I interrupted you while you were reading. I said, Hi, Honey, what are you doing? And you snapped at me. Why did you do that?

Because I was reading and you interrupted me. Why do you interrupt when you know it annoys me?

I was only being friendly. I called you Honey. Is that so terrible?

No, but an interruption is an interruption, friendly or unfriendly, Honey or Asshole.

You see? I try to be nice, call you Honey and so forth, and you think, it's a joke.

Notice the face, I reply. It's not smiling. Mouth isn't upturned, eyes uncrinkled, no ivory showing. Am I smiling?

Stop being cute, she says. You interrupt me when I'm reading and that's okay, right? To interrupt *me*. That's somehow different.

Sorry, I won't interrupt if you return the favor. Ouch! That little kid just banged into me. Stop a minute.

It was only a little kid. How could a little kid running into you hurt? You are such a baby. She looks into the store window beside where we're standing.

He ran into my nuts is why. You wouldn't understand.

That's right. Getting hit in the nuts is a guy thing, I get it. A woman could never understand the pain of getting whacked in the nuts.

Like childbirth, I say. That's a girl thing. Each sex has something uniquely its own that the other has to accept on faith. It's what separates us into male and female, you know, into nuts and ovaries. Let's keep going. I'm okay now. I should have brought a cattle prod to keep the little bastards away. But look, can't we argue reasonably?

Of course, she replies. You start the argument and I'll decide if you're being reasonable.

Okay, I say. Let's make a list of things that annoy us. For example, being interrupted while reading really annoys me, but let's say it doesn't really annoy you. Continuing in this vein, you could then say yourself, okay, it doesn't really annoy me but I'll respect his annoyance and not do it. I could perform a similar act of courtesy for you, depending on what annoys you more than it does me. How does that sound?

It sounds like a sexist double standard to me. If I shouldn't interrupt you while you read, why should you be permitted to interrupt me?

Because it isn't as important to you as it is to me. I'll then do the same for you. *Quid pro quo*. How is that a double standard?

Well, you're wrong. Don't try those goddamn double standards on me anymore. Hold on. Let's get an ice cream.

We go into the Ice Creame Shoppe. She orders chocolate, I get vanilla. You see, I remark, we can't even agree on the same flavor of ice cream.

She licks hers, then she licks mine. Sure we can, she says. Yours is better, so we both like vanilla. Let's trade, and she removes the vanilla cone from my hand and replaces it with the chocolate cone, neither of which I've yet had a chance to lick. You see? I'm easy to get along with, she says.

Good, I say. Then you won't interrupt me when I'm reading?

I didn't mean that, she answers slyly.

What exactly did you mean?

She gooses me and says, I mean that next time you should order strawberry.

Why so, I say.

Because, she says, it's another of my favorite flavors.

The Sometime
Bass with the Goodly Set

HE WAS ALL ANGLES and points and no rounded corners. He had lean hair and see-through teeth and in his youth had been known to preach some. For a time he took up serpents with the congregation over in Jolo where anointed ones speak in tongues, prophesying from the depths of strange magnetic fields and shouting out Scripture, Luke in particular, as snakes drip from their limbs like scaled kudzu: *Behold, I give unto you power to tread on serpents and scorpions, and over all the power of the enemy, and nothing shall by any means hurt you.*

West Virginia lacks neither serpents nor enemies, but has no scorpions. Still, they get by in Jolo, and on that night when the elders stiffened and looked past him, Wallace knew he was no longer in the Word. Following the single drum roll and a scree up the frets by the guitar player, after the chorus of amens affirming his lost soul, he came away minus Jesus with a snake-bit thumb that he sacrificed later to gangrene.

Right now his main concern was starting the outboard and adjusting the mix, a nine-fingered job to which Wallace displayed the usual stoop of impoverishment. There was the cussing, of course.

Onely felt good, like he could have loped all morning under cloud shadows. It must be the Prozac, he thought. He wondered if he would get any sleep with Wallace's stone-bent aluminum skiff wallowing on top of the waterweed like a drowned and bloated hog. A nap was likely impossible, but he was ready to make do. Making do was what he did best.

Onely was rumored to be overly fat, slow of movement, shiny and brown of eye—as Wallace put it, eyes like a couple of wet turds. But Onely cared little about what Wallace thought or said, and rumors passed across him like distorted echoes barely heard. He felt satisfied inside his eyes, thinking he was well hidden there. A pension out of the mines put food on the table and paid for the cable TV, and a man couldn't expect much more. Still, he regretted with a joyless decrepitude all he had missed in life, whatever that was.

A bullfrog grumped from the bank. On the stern seat Wallace answered with a belch. "I used to be a church-goer," he said, feathering the pull choke with this thumbless hand. "Yessir, I was, but I ain't anymore.." He wiggled his ears and seemed horsey and contented despite this confession that was not new. Onely asked himself from which dead menagerie of equine shapes, which peeling merry-go-round, Wallace had arisen incarnate and two-legged, dressed in coveralls that could have fit him double.

When they first met in '48, Onely told Wallace how things happened to his family in threes of multiples thereof, and Wallace laughed until he cried. "Your names *Onely Twice*?" His face could be a varicosity even then, run to coarseness by excessive masturbation and the desire to think in parables.

Onely had looked back puzzled as if seeing a Chinaman, but it was true. His Uncle Melvin Twice had weighed three hundred pounds and at his funeral six men were needed to lift the coffin. When a mine timber fell on his daddy's foot that foot swole up three times its natural size and cost his daddy three toes. To this day his baby brother Thrice won bets with those three nipples of his, and in '33, Natchez, one of his three sisters, gave birth to triplets. Two died right off, a fact never mentioned by Onely out of a lurking respect for symmetry.

Wallace untied the stern line holding them to the dock and edged the skiff around the lake parallel to the bank. A cloud of vapid blue exhaust hung beside their faces like personal gas. Their favorite bass hole was maybe fifteen minutes away if the mix was right, although Wallace liked running rich. Usually the engine died like a shot duck, and they sat drifting while Wallace yanked the starter cord, worked the choke like a plunger, and wondered loudly if Mr. Evinrude's parents had ever married.

It was nearly noon, late for bass but not for brim. To Onely a punkinseed was better than getting skunked. Wallace, of course, disagreed. He was a bass man all the way. To him, pan fishing was for pussies.

"I'm dropping iron up beside that patch of spadderdock," Wallace announced. The boat was his, leaving Onely no say in the matter. Not that he cared. Anyway, it was where they always anchored.

"Got me a new mail order reel," Onely said.

Wallace eyed Onely's shiny Shimano as if it might be venomous. "Never figured you to go Jap," and he spat for emphasis. "I fought the Japs in the Great War." But Onely knew that Wallace had been a guard at a Japanese-American internment camp in California, and the only fighting he had done was in the barracks.

Such could not be said of Onely, returning from a hitch in the same war too distant from his special history ever to relive it. Having found the world, he lost his place in it, the confidence of belonging somewhere, and was forever after a nomad in his own house. Erma Jean, half crippled with arthritis and mean as a fire ant, treated him like a boarder, hooting at him from the couch to carry her plate to the sink and wash it. Their yellow cat watched indifferently, sopping up and savoring its own selfishness, nurturing the greater challenge of mice.

His retirement revolved around changing rolls of toilet paper and flicking light switches. She nagged him into cleaning the wallpaper with stuff resembling modeling clay that picked up the dirt and held it, telling him always about the coal dust settling off his clothes those many years coming home from the mines. He meekly obeyed, still resigned not to be an inheritor of the Earth. New wallpaper would have been quicker, but Erma Jean loved her tiny pink rosebuds, and by acquiring the new she might have missed out on the torment of monotony. When he complained about how his wife treated him, Wallace smirked and replied, "A man your age and still pussy-whipped." Onely guessed it was true, although pussy was not a subject that came often to mind.

They stopped and anchored. Onely peered down to where strands of hornwort wriggled greenly, the rumpled surface cutting apart their stems and rejoining the ends with an oscillatory rhythm. Brim beamed up at him all sappy, like expectant commuters.

Wallace was rigging his casting rod. Onely watched without interest, having rigged his own before they left the dock. He thought lots about different things, usually ideas he got from reading at the public library over in Bluefield where he went often when the weather was too rainy or cold for fishing, or simply to avoid Erma Jean. Just yesterday he had read an article in a travel magazine. The trip took nine hours by jet plane and that was *after* you got to New York City.

Onely spied a message there and settled himself more comfortably on the bow seat. He could do this now that the boat had stopped moving. "I hate traveling nowadays," he said, even though he never did. "Traveling's easy on the young, but men our age carry the awful burden of stool softeners and suppositories and foot powder. Nitro tablets." He didn't mention Prozac, which was making him dizzy in the heat. During his last checkup the doctor had told him that he might be depressed, and Onely supposed it was true.

Wallace snorted. "When's the last time you traveled?"

"I don't recall, but me and Erma Jean went to Charleston back some time to get her arthuritis looked after." Following a pause, "We took the train." Wallace knew about that trip. He'd known since it happened twenty years before.

"The Lord God never promised you a rose garden," he snapped.

Onely pulled his belly up nearer to his belt and watched Wallace's spit spread mayonnaise-fashion across the water.

"I see you got new thread too," Wallace remarked. "That come with the reel?"

"Excalibur Silver. Bought it separate and wound it myself. 'That's how you survive the jungle,'" Onely quoted by memory from the original carton. "And new crankbaits, self-suspending. Excalibur Fat Free Shads."

Wallace waved a hand Onely's way and turned his head in disgust. "Well, shit, them bass don't stand a chance against you. No sense in me dropping this old spotted popper over." Onely knew Wallace was relishing the chance to test whose equipment was superior, and if Onely caught more fish Wallace would blame it on "advanced technology."

Onely crossed his hands over his belly and considered Erma Jean's admonishment about all literature except the Scripture being gates to trespass. Ever dutiful, he always opened the Holy Book first on settling into a chair at the library, wandering into Biblical deserts alongside raving prophets, marveling at the opaque teachings of Jesus and emerging from the Four Gospels as if from a thick sandstorm. A thought floated past, and his mind rose to the bait: had Jesus been a committee of scribes unable to reach consensus? Who else except a committee could have rolled away the stone?

When that slipped the hook, Onely said, "I read at the library that fish can see colors, and colors on a lure make a difference."

Wallace considered. "It don't make any difference because the Lord God put fish here on Earth for mankind's use. It's His way.

"I thought you wasn't religious anymore."

"I ain't, but a man still needs reasons for what he sees."

There was a hiatus while they each considered what the other had said—or didn't consider it, in Wallace's case.

"I see you still got on your Jesus belt buckle," Onely said, his lips barely lifting in what passed for a smile.

"Goddammit, don't dig at me, Onely. You know this buckle was give to me by Bernice." To regain the offensive Wallace peered into Onely's open tackle box and said with a smirk, "Got you some new ballhead jigs."

Onely leaned forward with effort, gasping out a mighty grunt as his diaphragm folded double, and took out a paper bag. "Yep, and here's others." He rummaged in the bag, extracting a mass of tiny jigs, their hooks entwined. "This here's a aspirin-style Buck Shot, a Tear Drop called a Thunderhawk Talon Tear, and two Bullet Jigs." He held two other jigs against the sun, one between each thumb and forefinger, and examined them minutely through bifocals as if they were rare gems. This one's a Blue Fox Foxee and over here we got us a Lindy Quiver."

"You aiming to demolate the whole damn brim population?"

"I am and I will," Onely answered firmly, "but I'll leave enough to multiply their kind." He could talk back like this to Wallace even if he couldn't to Erma Jean. It was enormously satisfying.

As if reading his mind, Wallace spoke and said, "Yessir, I reckon they's two differences amongst us, Mr. Twice: I ain't the one in this boat that's pussy-whipped, if you collect my message, and I ain't the one that's about to get skunked on bass this day." He cast his faded leopard-frog popper up against the spadderdock and gave a tug to start it swimming home.

Erma Jean didn't approve of Bernice and Wallace living in sin, but Onely didn't care. Having earlier deposited his DNA into several willing vessels, Wallace had allotted to Bernice the task of eventually burying him. At seventy-nine, he was twenty years her senior. Bernice had come to hold Onely in low regard ever since he told Wallace about the South Pacific islands, where in olden times dead chieftains were cast adrift on ocean currents in their royal canoes. Now Wallace insisted that Bernice bury him in his bass boat, and she had family to consider.

Bernice was odd-looking, resembling the mismatched halves of a thin woman and a fat one. From the waist up she was spare and bony as a winter tree, her collagen plus whatever fat and life's juices she had accumulated having sunk to the bottom and pooled there. In their house, where outside shadows bent darkly against the musty curtains, Wallace forced the stump of his thumb against Bernice's cracked lips in the morning and again at night. Those who get snake-bit are not in the Word because they failed to carry Jesus. At Jolo, Wallace handled serpents on faith alone, not as under an anointing when the divine hand nudges aside reptilian instinct and the flesh can't be harmed. That bite was coming. Jesus knew, and so had the congregation. Now Bernice suffered for it.

Onely considered lowering his jig into the water, but the effort seemed too much. He looked over the lake instead and saw a tapering shape not far in front of the boat. The object appeared to be sculling in place, pale against the deep of the lake, neither rising nor sinking, rolling partway over as if looking up at him. There could be no bigger bass anywhere, and it had to be albino.

"I see the biggest bass since the world's creation," Onely said softly.

After a moment Wallace answered without turning around. "I'd call that a *sometime* bass 'cause you think you see it sometimes when you don't. It ain't there, Onely. They ain't a bass in this whole lake bigger'n two pound."

Onely looked again, squinting to focus better. The object sank slowly, drifting toward the dark bottom before being grabbed by hidden eddies and shifting like a sheet of newspaper blown through an alley. And then it disappeared. Onely sat up and stared at the back of Wallace's cap where a horsefly prospected carefully, considering where to sink its shaft. He was rigged for jigging brim; changing over to a bass rig would require some effort.

"Goddammit, don't be shaking the boat," Wallace admonished. "I think I got me a trailer here, just inside the spadderdock." Sure enough, a small bass edged out of the weeds, showing interest in the popper.

Onely decided not to mention what he had seen, not out of selfishness but because a fish to Wallace was simply a trophy, something to brag about, and the bigger the fish the bigger the brag. Wallace had no aptitude for the mystical responsibilities of fishing.

Onely looked down again, this time nearer the bow, seeing the deeper hornwort forest arise undulating out of the polysaprobic ooze. He watched for a while, mesmerized by the swaying, not thinking about anything in particular. Strung at the end of his Silver Thread by a couple of hook knots and hanging off the last eye of the rod was a shiny Turner Jones Micro Guppy, looking like itself alone. A what-the-hell feeling came on him, and without moving his bulk he lowered the jig over the side. Nothing happened, either above or below. Every so often Wallace's plug bit discreetly into the water; hovering squadrons of dragonflies arrived. A horsefly fed from between his sweating shoulders, but he ignored the pain. The jig rose and fell, too new and obscene for the brim, which eyed it suspiciously as residents anywhere will eye the foreigner.

Onely felt light in the head, and his arms and chest seemed to bear a great weight of time. Anticipating what? The day became suddenly hotter. Must be the Prozac, he thought, but the view had also become strangely hazy. Lake and sky joined, their edges held together by the stitching of trees.

He looked down again. From the dark water rose an image that grew larger and brighter, separating abruptly from the curtain of the lake. Onely was astonished. It was a drowned white girl with hornwort hair, green and trailing. Except for the hair she was pale beyond belief, like snow. Her lips brushed the jig, but hers were not disturbing motions. Nothing she did glittered the surface. No, she must be alive, he thought, because her movements came too quick for the dead. She somersaulted as if in play, arching over backward and stretching toward him an enormous set of breasts, alabaster as the rest of her and the size of cantaloupes. No smile crossed the mouth, the eyes seemed blind and colorless without irises.

Onely felt disembodied, as if sinking into himself, hearing behind his ears a drumming like heartbeats gaining distance.

"I seen something peculiar," he said hoarsely.

"You ain't seen shit," Wallace replied without looking back. "Now shut and fish."

Onely, the final snapshot of that goodly set lying wet and undeveloped on his brain, sagged back. Abruptly the absence of sound and light came as a sublimation. Time drifted and the bass rose no higher, avoiding open water as if fearful of sunburn. Still facing the stern, Wallace sang the Oscar Meyer wiener song. The squadrons of dragonflies departed on another mission, but green-bottle flies were just arriving, having discovered in the lolling tongue a disguised entrance ramp to a new nursery. Still earlier arrivals, resplendent in iridescent chitin, were measuring the space between adenoids, possibly for French doors.

It's true that a man weighs more dead. At the dock they needed three strong men to get Onely out of that bass boat and six to lift the coffin on Saturday.

An Old Man
with Big Hands

HE WAS AN OLD man sitting in a wooden chair outside the Smoke-house Grill. We noticed his hands right away because they looked like they could squeeze the air out of a basketball. They were pale with rough yellow nails and brown liver spots and strawberry-blonde hairs sticking through the skin like hog bristles. They cupped a mouth harp so completely that not any part of it was visible. The old man was playing the mouth harp to entertain himself. It had to be just for himself because no one else was there. Not until we came around the corner. Not unless you counted his dog, which was asleep in the sun and didn't seem to be listening.

We stopped to hear, but it was an unfamiliar hillbilly tune. The old man glanced up and his eyes smiled. The eyes were all we could see of his face; his hands covered the rest. He was wearing a tattered straw hat that he maybe shared with a plow mule, and his clothes were so loose they didn't seem to touch him anywhere. He was small except for the hands, a shrunken old man with big hands sitting in the May sunshine.

He stopped playing and took his hands away from his face, but the mouth harp still didn't appear. It stayed submerged in the depth of his palm where we couldn't see it. He appraised us shrewdly, squinting one-eyed against the sun. "Y'all skipping school?"

We looked at our feet and pawed the sidewalk until JR said, "Yep. We're going for a swim up Rock House Road." Of the three of us JR was tallest, but he walked stooped over. His complexion was bad and he grimaced all the time. On JR's face laughing and crying looked the same. My ma said this was because he had a hidden sadness. He didn't have a first name, just the initials J and R.

"Go to school," the old man said. His dog got up slowly and stretched, pushing out its forelegs and poking its shaggy rump in the air. It yawned mightily and shook itself as dogs do when they're covered with water, although this dog was dry.

"What for?" Larry said. Larry had a pinched face like a squirrel's and squinted all the time. My ma said it was because he needed glasses. Even if he did Larry's family could never afford to buy them. There were eight kids at home, and his dad working shift. My only recollection of Larry's ma is of her sitting in a chair nursing a baby. She always looked wilted, like flowers in a vase when someone forgets to add water. She seemed to be an endless source of babies. They emerged from her at regular intervals and grew into dirty little pinch-faced kids. The yard was filled with them. They would watch silently as I walked up to the door. I never learned their names.

"If you don't go to school you got to work the mines," the old man said. He patted his dog's head. "Then you get black lung like me and can't do nothing at all."

"Miners make good money," JR said. "It's where I'm heading soon as I turn sixteen in two years."

The old man shook his head as the old do upon hearing the wisdom of the young. He stuck a massive hand against his face and music emerged from underneath it. The dog lay back down. It sighed and closed its eyes.

The old man stopped playing and took away his hand so he could speak. Your name's JR, ain't it," he said. It wasn't a question.

"That's me," said JR. He grimaced more than usual and looked at the old man curiously, as if trying to remember something from a long time back. The old man resumed playing. He closed his eyes to make us disappear.

"Let's go," I said. Larry and I had come into Man that morning on the pretext of going to school, but when the school bus made a last stop before Man Junior High we got off. JR met us there. JR lived in town, a few blocks from school. We were on the way to his house to see if his ma might have left a pack of cigarettes lying around. A smoke tasted good after swimming. JR's little brother was in class and his ma would be working. JR didn't have a daddy, at least not that he ever mentioned. His ma had always talked about moving to Huntington, but now she thought Richmond might be better. In the end they didn't go anywhere.

We went into his ma's bedroom. It had the usual woman stuff spread here and there. Underwear and stockings were draped across the bed and wadded up on the floor. Shoes were lined up underneath the bed with the heels sticking out, some tipped onto their sides. The bed hadn't been made. We opened her dresser drawers and looked in the night stand but couldn't find any cigarettes. We searched the living room too. JR finally found an unopened pack of Lucky Strikes hidden in the sugar canister in the kitchen. We each made a sandwich out of bread and ketchup and wrapped them in toilet paper. There wasn't anything to put inside the bread. We stuck the sandwiches in our pockets and went outside.

The morning was hot. We walked through town and held out our thumbs. Two men in a bucking pickup stopped and asked where we were headed. We told them Rock House Road. They said they were going that way and to climb in back. They carried us through Long Bottom to where Rock House Road diverts from the hard road and starts up the mountain. We jumped out and said much obliged. They nodded and drove away.

Rock House Road was unpaved. It switch-backed up the mountain, at times becoming a leafy tunnel. Yellow poplars, oaks, and maples towered overhead, their foliage covered with gray dust thrown up from the roadbed. Halfway up was a mine. Past the mine was a quarry where limestone had been removed. The limestone had been pulverized and sprinkled onto the floor of the mine to cover coal spills and coal dust and reduce the chances of fire from sparking machinery. After being abandoned the quarry filled with water from underground springs. The water was clear and icy cold all year. Hardly anyone went there.

We walked in sweaty silence. At the quarry we stripped naked, climbed onto a large flat boulder, and dived in. The temperature change was so startling that we sprang back through the surface gasping and yelling. I was the best swimmer. I ducked underwater and pulled JR down by his ankles.

"Goddamn you!" he sputtered as our heads emerged. "Cut it out or I'll stomp you flat!"

"Who's gonna help you?" I leered, turning attention to Larry, who dog-paddled furiously to shore and scrambled onto the boulder.

"Come on up," Larry said. He was standing on solid ground and beckoning me closer. "Come on up so I can kick your ass."

I inched forward and made a grab for his ankles, but JR could stand now and got me in a headlock from behind. Larry jumped in to join JR, and they punched me several times before letting go. We splashed and punched each other some more before climbing onto the boulder and spreading out. The sun was hot on my face and chest, and the warm rock felt good against my back. JR peeled open the Luckies and passed around the pack. We lit up.

"You asshole," JR said to me. "You could of drowneded me. I ain't that good a swimmer."

"You oughta be drowneded 'cause you're such a ugly bastard," Larry said. "Your mama would thank us." I shaded my eyes and glanced sideways. Larry was grinning at me. I sat up.

"Sandra called me last night," I said.

"Hey, that's good," JR said. He sat up. Larry sat up too. None of us had any experience with girls, but we talked as though we did. We talked about girls and cars and sports. There wasn't anything else worth talking about.

"So what did she say?" Larry asked.

"She'd come over to the coal camp to see her sister, the one that's married. Said she'd be walking down the tracks past my house. That I ought to come outside and walk her back to her sister's."

"Did you?" JR asked. There was tension in his voice.

"Yeah," I said. "It was dark. I kissed her and grabbed a feel besides."

"Really?" I could tell Larry was impressed.

"She's got some big 'uns," JR offered. He was right. Sandra was only fourteen the same as us, but certainly far along in development. She had dark hair and dark eyes and a dead brown tooth in front, although the tooth didn't detract very much from her overall good looks.

"I got to be careful talking on that damned party line," I said. "You can never tell who might be listening in."

"What's she say that you gotta be so careful?" said JR.

I rolled onto my stomach. "She says that if me and her was boyfriend and girlfriend I could touch her more, but she won't let me do it if I don't commit. That's the kind of stuff she says on the party line."

Larry said, "I think you oughta commit."

"Me too," JR echoed, "unless your too stupid to see the advantages."

They were right, of course, but it was easy for them to say. The disadvantage was being teased continuously at school, hearing your friends saying in sing-song voices, "Here comes little Sandra with the great big 'uns." That and stuff like "When y'all getting married?" I could do without it. The best situation would be a secret girlfriend I wouldn't have to commit to but who would let me touch her. Maybe a girl from another school.

"I got to think on it," I said.

JR said, "Larry, he really is a dumbass. Let's drown him." They jumped on me and rolled me off the boulder into the water, then jumped in themselves, but I was too good a swimmer and got away easily. We horsed around a while, then climbed out and lay in the sun to dry off. We ate our sandwiches and had another smoke.

"What time you figure it is?" JR was shading his eyes with one hand and looking into the sun.

"About two," Larry said. "Time to go."

We dressed and hiked down to the hard road. The walking was easier going downhill. We thumbed a ride back to Man with some miners. They dropped us in front of the Smokehouse. The old man was gone. So was his dog. The chair wasn't there either.

"Let's go in and shoot some pool," JR suggested. "I got twenty-five cents. Larry had some change in his pocket, and so did I. The legal age to enter an establishment that served alcohol was eighteen, but no one in Man much cared in 1956.

The owner saw us come in, and a few regulars turned to look us over. Most were miners off shift or former miners retired or on disability. We racked the balls and argued over who got to break. We were playing eight ball; only two could play at a time, unless you were playing partners, then four could play. I said I'd sit out the first game and play the winner.

The owner came over. "Y'all want a short beer?"

I said, "We ain't got any money, just got enough to shoot pool."

The owner was sympathetic. "That's okay," he said. "Y'all my future customers." He grinned a toothless grin and spit a stream of tobacco juice onto the floor. Then he brought us three foaming shorts. JR got out the pack of Luckies, and we lit up. When JR picked up the cue ball it disappeared completely in his hand. I'd never noticed how big his hands were. Truly gigantic.

"Look at JR's hands," I said to Larry, who was leaning on his cue stick waiting to beak.

"What about them? They're ugly just like the rest of him."

"No, I mean, they're really big," I insisted. "Like that old man's hands. The old man playing the mouth harp."

"Yeah, I never seen him around here before, nor that dog neither. You ever seen him JR?"

JR straightened up. He set the cue ball on the table and stuck his hands in his pockets. "You break," he said to Larry.

Larry looked confused. "You won the toss, shithead. You called heads and it was heads, so you get to break."

"Y'all play," JR said. His voice sounded small and far away. He kept watching the door as if waiting for someone to come in, but no one did. He just stood there. He wouldn't look at us or take his hands out of his pockets.

Home is the Sailor,
Under the Sea

HE WAS A SAILOR retired from the sea, but not its rhythmic heaving, the circadian pulse of its tides. Objects washed up in the night collected at his doorstep like disassembled memories. In the fragments of shells and bits of seaweed lurked a damp emptiness similar to his own. Their immobility mocked him; their silence reminded him of his own death, so that he was forced to look away.

His personal history had vanished into a dry haze. Darkness became intolerable. He slept in fitful disharmony, stepping easily into his dream until sleep and wakefulness were the same. Hiiaka always appeared, her black hair sliding away into indigo. Countless times he reached over the side, grasping nothing. Frantic, he jumped overboard, pulling hand over hand down shafts of moonlight, through tremulous bubbles that wobbled out of the abyss. He touched one just as a cloud obscured the moon. The handholds dissolved; he floated up, feeling the sea's lessening weight on his lungs. Upon regaining the air imploding echoes of failure and loss passed between his lips, and he awoke with a howl, skin tingling as if abraded against the darkness.

At other times the sounds and images—even the sight of his own hands—assumed dreamlike qualities. Put away after one dream the bent fingers unfolded like stiff flowers in the next, and on through an endless sequence of wakefulness masquerading as sleep. He watched as his hands, without any apparent instructions, baited hooks, opened coconuts, pounded breadfruit pulp. If he muttered surprise the other villagers laughed and shook their heads.

Once in the thin darkness before dawn his mind suddenly cleared. The dream had released him. Overhead a gray lizard stalked a moth along the roof supports. Awareness and recognition fused once again; here was correlation of life with movement. He turned sideways. Pale light seeping through holes in the thatch settled on the hut's sandy floor, cratering his footprints in shadow. Silhouettes of palms creaking and shivering in the doorway sprang pertinaciously from memory, their shapes at once familiar. The land odors were sharp, as if he had been away at sea; they told him it was late spring. He must act quickly before the haze returned and stole his mind.

Outside, objects of daily use seemed clean and bright, as if freshly washed. He glanced around trying to recall their histories. Did they belong to him or to others? What others? Indistinct images of relatives and friends appeared before him, but time had passed. Their faces seemed young, too young. Perhaps they had moved to other islands; maybe they were dead.

He walked to the beach where his canoe lay tethered like a beached turtle to a coconut palm. Its stern held a silver pool of rainwater. In its surface he saw a wrinkled face with rheumy eyes, framed by long white hair. The eyes smarted, releasing unsuspected feelings. He knuckled them roughly, but the image hung pale and ghostly behind his eyelids as if frozen in a lightning flash. The years had left without him, like birds lifting into the wind.

Behind his hut, in a clearing filled with sunlight, he built a drying rack on which he laid slices of plantain and coconut. The giant breadfruit tree nearby was heavy with fruit oozing white sap. He picked several and baked them in his earthen oven, afterward removing skin and seeds and pounding the pulp with a club dipped frequently in water. The doughy pulp was laid in sheets across the rack to dry. He discovered several sweet potatoes cached in the cool ground underneath the hut. He baked then sliced most of them, and set the slices on the rack.

Voices drifted from the village, but he had no wish to visit. He could smell cooking fires and hear children laughing. Constructing the drying rack and preparing the fruits and vegetables had taken all day. In the failing light he crafted fishing lures from pieces of sea turtle shell. When it became too dark to see he ate a cold sweet potato and went to sleep.

He awoke again before dawn. From coconut husks scattered on the ground he pulled fibers and twisted them into string by rolling them against his thigh. The finished strings he spliced end to end and braided into a rope that he soaked in the sea to toughen. Other coconut fibers were dipped in breadfruit sap and pounded into cracks in the hull of the canoe. He leveled the canoe and filled the hull with seawater so the wood would swell, pressing the edges of the cracks against the new fibers to form tight seals. When night came he began weaving a sail from pandanus leaves, relying in the absence of illumination on knowledge stored in his fingers.

After three days he bailed out the canoe, attached the sail to the mast, retied the outrigger using his new rope, and put to sea. The hull did not leak, and the new sail, stiff and dry, crackled and chattered. He tightened the lines, tacking back and forth across the wind, laughing and wiping spray from his face. After catching a *máhimáhi* by trolling with his lures he returned to the beach. He cut the fish into thin slices that he soaked in seawater before smearing them with their own blood and spreading them on the drying rack.

In the afternoon he collected other provisions: coconuts, both green and ripe, lengths of fishing twine, and empty coconuts in which to store drinking water. These last he filled through their open eyes and sealed shut with coconut fiber dipped in breadfruit sap. Two would be needed for each day at sea unless there was rain.

He was conscious now that his back hurt. Squatting for long periods numbed his legs. When kneeling before the earthen oven his knees seemed filled with the spines of sea urchins. He remembered none of this pain from before. Perhaps it was better to live thoughtlessly, confined like a beast within his cage of dreams.

The oven needed fuel. Grunting, cradling an armload of drift-wood, he gauged the distance back to the hut. . . too far; the load was too big. With another grunt he dropped everything, assembled a more modest burden, and trudged on through the sand. Yes, he decided, pain was preferable to not feeling. Before, each day had rolled under him like a sea swell, rising and falling yet staying in place while the sea's energy rushed past. His life had risen and fallen with the days, leaving him soaked and dying, no closer to Hiiaka. Now he could go; the knowledge was still there. As a young man they had called him *ho'okele*, or sailing master.

There were certain protocols, although he no longer cared. The *kilo hoku* from the village might consent to bless his trip, but at the cost of considerable distraction. Other villagers would question his motive or sanity; even worse, someone might ask to come along. He could have baked a pig if he owned one, or chewed and mixed *'awa*, but so little time remained. At any moment the haze could return and steal his thoughts. So he scanned the sea and sky for signs of bad weather, seeing no unusual wave formations or bro-ken clouds rushing before a storm. The sea was nearly flat, and the only clouds were *newe-newe*, puffy on top with their yellow bellies pressed against the horizon.

His course would be south and slightly east; the altitude of the fixed star *Hokupa'a*, from where he stood, was two fists above the horizon. As he crossed the invisible boundary separating the north-ern and southern worlds *Hokupa'a* would lie directly on top of the sea. He had made this trip several times, but always in a large dou-ble-hulled canoe with many others. The journey had taken thirty to forty days in each direction, depending on winds and currents. When he left he would be sailing against both.

Two weeks passed, and everything was ready. In his last dawn ashore he loaded the canoe, covering the provisions with a tight-ly-woven mat of pandanus leaves to protect against sun and sea-spray. Food and water were sufficient for a month, and he would trail lures hoping for fresh fish. Nights would be cold and often wet, the days blistering unless there was cloud cover. Comfort mattered little. He thought instead about Hiiaka, who used to shiver when the sun rested even briefly behind clouds. If raindrops or a cool breeze touched her skin in the night she moved closer, absorbing his warmth. Before sleep she often rubbed her arms with crushed *pikake* blossoms. The scent rose between them, mingling with their heat like smoke from a hidden fire. He smelled it now, as he had that morning upon awakening to see the lizard watching him.

Overnight an offshore wind had flattened the sea and bunched its surface into glittering bands made orange by the sun. Gills rose from the beach as he walked, appearing black and shapeless against the eastern sky. He untied the canoe and pushed its bow into the low surf. Sand and broken shells shifted under his feet, solid and reassuring. From the land itself he had taken only a large stone, little different from the other, that first stone. Without looking back he climbed aboard and paddled until clear of the low breakers, then raised the sail.

By afternoon his island had disappeared, although signs of its presence remained: drifting vegetation, a reef of high clouds, the swells pushing outward around invisible headlands. At evening flocks of *noio* heading back to shore after a day of fishing revealed how far he had traveled. At sunset he caught a *kāwakāwa* that he sliced into strips and ate raw with pieces of dried banana and breadfruit and washed down with a coconut shell of water.

In the darkness he held position by keeping *Hokupaʻa* behind him, tacking off course alternately to the southeast and southwest, but plunging ever southward. On each tack he napped, feeling in the sea's motion any deviation from the course. His body fell easily into the jostling of the swells, and he imagined himself cradled between the gigantic breasts of a sea goddess. Dozing, rousing himself in half-sleep to alter course slightly, he pressed a hand to his chest. Soon he would put his ear to Hiiaka's as she slept, hearing behind her flesh and ribs the echoes of his own heart.

In the morning a flock of *manu-a-ku* passed overhead, sunlight glancing off their white plumage. They dipped and swirled. He watched, estimating the distance he had traveled. Like the *noio* the *manu-a-ku* return to land each evening, but the *manu-a-ku* travel three times farther out to sea. If the wind held he would not be seeing them tomorrow.

After tying off the lines he baited two lures with strips of skin from the *káwakáwa* caught the previous day and trailed them off the stern within easy reach. The morning sky portended no rain. For breakfast he ate dried plantain and coconut and drank a coconut shell of water. He thought about saving the empty vessel to fill with future rainwater, but instead watched it bob away among the fluid blue hills. He stood and urinated over the side, thinking of the wasted water in his stream. The *manu-a-ku* did not require freshwater, nor did the fishes beneath him; only humans needed it. Eventually he would sink like a fish into the sea's dim canyons, hearing no sound, seeing no sun. From down there the splash of a man's urine must sound like rain falling on a roof, insignificant as raindrops.

There was nothing to do except maintain course and check the baits. During the day he marked his course by the sun. At night the stars rose at known location on the eastern horizon and set at known places in the west. As a young man he had been taught to use a star compass with sixteen points around the horizon. Each point represented the middle of a house of the same name. East is *hikina*, or "arriving," where the sun and other stars arrive on the horizon. West is *komohana*, or "entering," where the sun and other stars enter the horizon. North is *'akau*; south is *hema*. . . He knew the rising and setting places of the stars in the different houses of the sky. As he traveled south and crossed the line that separates north from south their rising and setting points would shift southward, and the farther south he sailed the greater the shift would become. The moon rises and sets every night in a different place, but with knowledge a sailing master could use the moon to hold course. He knew these things. They were no less familiar than his thumbnails, yellowed and ridged as the backs of old seashells.

In the beginning there had been no light, only darkness. The progenitors—Rangi our father, Papa our mother—lay together inseparable, Heaven and Earth. Their six sons grew tired of eternal darkness and discussed whether to kill their parents, but one brother, Tane-mahuta, father of the forests and all that inhabit them, lobbied to pry them apart. At last, five of the six agreed with this plan, and one by one they tried, but their parents were too vast. Then it was Tane-mahuta's turn, and with a mighty effort he separated Rangi and Papa. At that moment numerous human beings became visible, having been concealed until then.

But Tawhiri-ma-tea, father of winds and storms, had never agreed to the plan, fearing his kingdom would be destroyed and the world would become sunny and beautiful. Instead he rose Heavenward with Rangi, his father, becoming lost in the anonymity of stars. There Tawhiri-ma-tea produced many offspring, including those he sent to the north, east, south, and west, giving them names of those winds, but keeping for himself the mightiest of winds, the cyclone.

The progeny of Tawhiri-ma-tea lurk in rain squalls, waterspouts, clouds of all colors and shapes, thunderstorms. Before Tawhiri-ma-tea's fury even Tangaroa, father of the oceans and all that live in them, hides in the deep for safety. These and similar conflicts became the way of the world, and so it has been ever since. Despite everything, Heaven and Earth are still in love. When Papa sighs, the mist rising toward Heaven is her bosom; and as Rangi bemoans the loss of his wife, the tears he lets fall from his eyes we call the dew.

Can you hear their voices? I hear murmurs, whispers, muffled weeping. I remember from the time before the haze, the time of memory. I must turn away, ignore them, the parents of my race. Have I too become a god? A voice hasn't any weight or substance; it leaves no imprint, no sign of its passing. Voices falter on air; the wind erases them. They were never here.

Under me are drowned women, half fish now. I know; I've seen them. One surfaced many years ago while my companions slept. Our canoe was becalmed, and I stood alone under the jabbering sail. She stuck her head up and looked directly at me, eyes reflective and hopeless as those of a fish, her mocking smile evoking in me a deep sorrow. Is that all? I thought. If I tumble overboard and drown will my legs fuse at the knee and ankle? Will my feet curve back, becoming a crescent like the tail of an *ahi*? And which will I be upon arriving at that endless banquet under the sea, pursuer or pursued? Then she was gone, leaving a black circle in the moonlight. At dawn while the sailing master was taking his morning piss I described what I had seen. It was a woman's ghost, he replied, not a real woman. Perhaps a woman long since drowned, perhaps not. Who can tell? But I know what I saw: a ghost casts no shadow. There I go again, talking to myself. . .

Is it true? Are there lands elsewhere that are dry as dust, hot as an oven of stones in the ground? Are there places where men have never glimpsed the sea? Some say that across the world are islands so vast a war canoe sailing before the wind cannot pass around them, not even in a thousand days and nights. Such a thing, of course, is preposterous.

You are old and weak! screams the south wind. Little devils sent by Tawhiri-ma-tea, they're sneaking up from the port side along our western tack. Be careful, Hiiaka! Don't stand up, you might fall overboard! The wind strengthens; cold spray climbs over the gunwales and hurls itself against my skin like a shower of tiny stones. Hiiaka was there once, in my line of vision, hair flying outward between the mast and wind-driven sea. Her feet, unknown to me, rested on a stone that no one saw. Tangaroa dives under the keel and hides, the coward! Afraid of his own brother! I can't protect the gods from each other. . . And when I look up, she's gone.

He was suddenly aware of his finger coming into focus. Pointing. Admonishing the unseen. A remnant of something said before the shriek of a tern. So that's how it was: he shouted, birds replied. The haze had returned without warning, attacking silently like *niuhi* the maneater who leaves behind only dismembered scraps unfit except for scavengers. The mind stretches, extending distances between past and present before contracting and reassembling itself in a different form. Soon his two halves would pull apart like old rope, trailing the frayed ends of memory and recognition. Then he would be like the birds and fishes, able to find his way and feed himself, but no longer a child of the Ancestors.

How long had his mind been away? It was daylight, but which

day? After securing the sail he lifted the mat and took inventory of his stores. Since the last time he could recall he had eaten food for three days and drunk six coconut shells of water. The stone remained in place, dense and implacable. So. . . three days of bellowing at terns, of raging against *malolo* the flying fish. What a fool he was! He inspected the canoe, making minor repairs and adjustments and at sunset tacked southeast. The taller seas were now against his starboard bow. Soon *Hokupa'a* appeared over his left shoulder. He ate some dried fish and celebrated his mind's return by opening a green coconut.

The lures had not fished well in his absence, and he scolded himself. The bone hook was missing from one; the thin strip of fish skin dangling from the other was now several days old. No sensible fish would be interested. He tore it off and threw it away. After repairing the broken lure he decided to keep both aboard for the night to let them rest. Rejuvenated they would fish better at dawn.

He continued on the southeastern tack until the moon began to wane, then came about and headed southwest once again. In the night he started to shiver, but warmed quickly after eating some dried breadfruit. Even though he lived closer to the sea than to the clouds he was more like a bird than a fish. The blood of a bird is warm. Its heart pumps like a human heart. A fish's blood is always cold. Did fishes have hearts? Probably not, he thought, because then their blood would be warm too. The heart is the body's sun, and when the sun in the sky sets the blood is soon cooled despite efforts of that lesser sun beneath the ribs.

Against the pale streaks before sunrise he saw the stars *Ke Ali'i o Kona i ka Lewa* and *Puana-kau* set together. He was not quite halfway to the imaginary line separating the northern and southern worlds. When clouds later obscured the sky he held course by feeling the motion under him, knowing that ocean swells move directly from one house on the star compass toward another of the same name in the opposite quadrant.

The next day his lures caught three *opelu palahu*, which he ate raw with slices of dried sweet potato. The fresh food warmed his stomach. By mid-morning the warmth had spread to his back and knees. He felt young and supple. Hiiaka reminded him to keep his lures in the sea. Dried food will not sustain you, she admonished. Soon you and your food will look alike, wrinkled and unappealing. And then what? I'll tell you. No decent woman will have you, including me. He imagined the giggles that followed, the hand pressed to his cheek. Ha! He thought, she's right. He dutifully baited his lures with the shiny skin and entrails of the *opelu palahu* and tossed them into his wake.

The swells had grown. Dark clouds—*'ilio uli*— rose in the distance as if peering at him from over the edge of the world. Legs had descended from their bellies by afternoon, and they danced in a ragged line across the sky. He was reminded of the great battle once fought on his island between the gods. Tawhiri-ma-tea, appearing as a cyclone and driving rain before him, attacked Tane-mahuta, god of the forests and all that is made of wood. Great palms and breadfruit trees were ripped from the earth and hurled at one another; canoes were dashed against shoals of coral. Many people died, some crushed like insects as they fled into the writhing forest. Ever after Hiiaka trembled at the sound of thunder and ran to him for protection, hiding like a child against his chest.

Tawhiri-ma-tea came in the night. Putting his lips to the mast he moaned loudly. Tawhiri-ma-tea grabbed the sail at its edges and shook until it rattled and fought wildly against the lines. All around was blackness, like the dark that covered the world before Rangi and Papa were separated and light could fill the space between them. The sea spray felt unusually cold. He needed food, but the mat covering his stores was secured tightly.

Just as he untied it the sail line slipped through his other hand causing the canoe to lurch suddenly and lose its heading. With the outrigger momentarily submerged the hull corkscrewed, backing its stern into the swells and letting in the sea. He dropped the lines for fear the sail would rip away and began bailing with his hands, but for every handful thrown overboard two more took its place.

Tawhiri-ma-tea's voice had risen to a shriek, and the spray was now mixed with rain. Like living things the swells pressed their sides against the canoe and lifted it high onto their shoulders, releasing it to be gathered on the shoulders of others. It's a game, he thought, simply a game that will soon end. Tawhiri-ma-tea toys with me as a dog toys with a rat, and when the rat is dead the dog becomes bored.

As dawn arrived the rain slackened and stopped. The eastern sky just before sunrise held no hint of red patches that often signal more rain. Against the brightening sea hung long narrow clouds. Their edges pointed up, a sign of calm weather.

He was cold and very tired and welcomed the sun's heat on his skin. If only there were food. The storm had ripped away the pandanus mat over his provisions and washed them away. A few soggy pieces of sweet potato remained, but they would be too salty to eat. He finished bailing, leaving the remaining water to evaporate. The swells were still huge, but a gentle wind had softened their white tops. He refitted his lines, and the canoe hove to the southeast and into the rising sun.

On course once more he searched the canoe, finding two coconut shells filled with water and two ripe coconuts. And the stone, which not even the gods could eat. Without rain he would die of thirst. At least the lures were safe. He yanked the lines, feeling them dive into the wake. The flesh of fishes is less salty than the sea. You could eat a fresh fish without fear of dehydration. So his plan was simple: fish the lures day and night, hope for rain, and continue on a southward course.

As the swells diminished he compensated as usual for leeway by keeping the bow pointed as sharply as possible into the wind. In seas of reasonable size the sailing master can estimate leeway and compensate for leeward displacement by observing the angle between his heading and the wake of the canoe.

That night he sailed under clear skies, trailing lures that caught nothing. His stomach complained loudly about its lack of food. After taking two swallows of water he settled back to wait. Waiting was his only choice.

You are always impatient, Hiiaka scolded. He saw her bending at the waist and shaking her finger. So impetuous! The gods made you a mere mortal, not one of them, so be patient! Then she smiled. It's enough, he said to himself. Early next morning the stars *Ke Ali'i o Kona i ka Lewa* and *Hokulei* set together. He had moved closer to the invisible line dividing the northern and southern worlds.

When the sun was overhead he tacked again. Today the sun was unkind, paying no attention to his thirst. It burned ruthlessly, keeping the rain clouds away. He finished the half-empty coconut of water and tossed the vessel overboard. Only one remained. No birds crossed the sky; there were no sounds except the slosh of the sea against the hull and the clattering of the sail.

Just as the sun was disappearing he caught a *mâhimâhi*. It was a large male fish resplendent in greens and yellows. He killed it quickly and ate strips of flesh from its sides, saving the iridescent pieces of the bony head to bait his lures. In the fish's upper stomach was a fresh flying fish. He ate this too, savoring its oily taste. The meal alleviated some of his thirst and all of his hunger. He stored what was left of the fish underneath the pandanus mat and rinsed his hands in the sea. As he was starting to tack he heard Hiiaka asking, Does all food taste the same to you? It seems you swallow everything too quickly to taste it. Ah, but no matter, let me touch your cheek. Here, I've saved you an extra portion.

At dawn the next day he drank half the remaining water and ate most of the leftover fish. To ration was foolish, he told himself. He was old and needed strength to keep the canoe on course. And besides, the haze could return at any moment, then he would not know whether he was alive or dead, except in the way that a fish knows, or a bird. Incredibly he would not recognize his own hands and feet; his arms and legs would appear to him as mysterious as the stars. And his face, reflected in a quiet pool, would be that of a stranger, no one he had ever known. If the gods decided he should live, they would provide. If not. . .

The *newe-newe* that day hunkered low on the horizon. Perhaps they are resting from the heat, he told himself. Maybe they will call other clouds, and among these some might bring rain. It was water he needed most. He looked around. There were no vessels left in which to hold rainwater except the canoe itself. Were the rainstorm accompanied by strong wind and high seas, sea spray would poison the rainwater with salt. He hoped for a heavy rain with little wind.

Evening brought no sign of rain clouds. The last of the provisions had been consumed. He could do nothing except hold course and hope to arrive at his destination before death found him.

He felt disoriented. Hunger, he told himself. The sea sliding underneath caused him to lean more than usual; the jostling made staying seated difficult. His arms felt light, as if they could lift off at any moment, like the wings of a bird. Stand and soar! And why not? Was he not a child of the Ancestors? He stood suddenly releasing the sail line. The canoe skidded and spun, dipping its prow under the chin of a swell and causing him to come unbalanced and crack his head against the mast. Spots of color flashed like fireflies in the night sky.

He stumbled to the stern and grabbed the line, pulling the sail taut and forcing the canoe back on course. Stupid! he said to himself. The hunger did not matter, nor the loneliness. A man in a canoe has no companions. His fingers have each other; his hands, arms, legs are paired, not going anywhere without the other. Is the remaining arm of a one-armed man lonely? He could not know, having never met a one-armed man. Ah, but the head! The head is alone. Perhaps this explains the mind, why it questions, doubts, sees ghosts, turns delusional. Yes, those other parts of the body still function when his mind enters its fog: the legs surely walk, if aimlessly; the fingers splice line for no apparent purpose. They remember their tasks, even after the mind abandons them. But the mind can't be fooled. It knows that laughter is bereavement, that love is a form of dying.

In the night he passed the invisible boundary between north and south. *Hokupa'a* lay at eye level; two other stars, *Kaulia* and *Ka Mole Honua*, crossed low on the horizon in the southern sky. At dawn a great fish took one of the lures, breaking the line. His spares had been washed overboard in the cyclone; only one still trailed behind. Fish by yourself, he told it. Don't look to me for bait, just do your job. Either we catch a fish or we both die, and you will sink to the bottom too. The coral will grow on your shiny surfaces, turning them dull. Silt will bury you. He laughed out loud.

Morning came, and the sky was clear and hot. The sea spray felt good on his shoulders, like oven stones when raindrops strike them. . . water dripping from Hiiaka's fingers. . . the dew falling slowly off *pikake* blossoms. He must not think about water! Stupid! he said aloud, and beat the heel of his hand against his forehead. He tacked, not caring how far he had come on the present course, not caring. . .

We are alone inside ourselves. Truly alone. For a time, so short, we can touch others. When in love we think we know someone— think we can see inside another being but it's delusion, a dream. We touch as if dreaming. Five fingers, ten. Would twenty be better? This traveling and going nowhere; planning trips, never arriving.

It was my failing, not yours, my sterile seed sprayed against your fertile earth. No! I'm to blame, a barren rock swept clean. When your seed falls on mine I incinerate it; my womb is like hot lava. Nothing matters, not now.

The stone! Why did you do this, Hiiaka? We were going to a new land. The gods there are fertile, the women waddle down shady paths holding their bellies, men's penises drag along the round like Tangaroa's. Babies are conceived merely by touching, you'll see. So, why did you do this? You might have tried! Those silver bubbles crushed from your lungs by Tangaroa's hands, they were my last sight of you. When I touched them they came apart.

At sunset a brown moth landed on the side of the mast. It stayed there, hunkered down against the wind that tried to blow it back out to sea. What air currents had brought it? In the darkness he dozed, feeling the sea and relying on the swells to steer. His mind roamed. He awakened once again in his hut, seeing the moth over-head. The lizard's eye seemed empty of curiosity or pity. It was just an eye, unconnected to a mind. He awoke suddenly and reached for the moth, intending to eat it, but the moth was gone. Here he was, following the rhumb of a star that seemed no more real than his memory of Hiiaka.

The rain did not come, and without water his mind drifted, en-tering its fog more frequently and staying longer each time. Nothing could be done about it, although the course held. He passed the first

sea-mark, a place where sea jellies gathered in uncountable numbers. At night the surface glowed greenly with phosphorescence. As
his prow cleaved through them they shouted to him. Find her! She's
Tangaroa's wife now, but she waits for you. After all, Tangaroa has
many wives; he won't miss one, more or less.

That day he sailed through the sea of sharks, the second sea-mark.
In the low swells he could see their eyes reflecting sunlight, their
blue backs brightening the deeper indigo of the water. They swam
toward him from all around, jostling each other and bumping the
canoe. She's here! they said. We let her pass. Yes, she sank through
our midst with a stone tied to her ankle; it happened quickly. Let
her pass! Tangaroa had shouted from below, so we had no choice.
You may pass too. Sail on. You know the place.

In the night he entered the region of the third sea-mark where
flying fish flew only in pairs. The sky was clear, and under moonlight he saw them rise out of the sea, beating their fins like wings.
They spoke to him and said familiar things. Was it memory speaking or Hiiaka giving instructions? Two landed in the canoe. He
picked them up gently and dropped them overboard; these were
her messengers.

The next day the wind stopped completely, and the swells lay
down on their sides as if entering sleep. He recognized where he
was. By dawn of the next days the stars ʻAʻa and Nana-mua would set
together. He stood uncertainly, legs and back aching, and dropped
the sail line. The sail hung limply, like a broken bird. Now he would
wait. The haze came once more, and he entered it gladly. At dusk the
dolphins appeared, his fourth and last sea-mark. They swam around
the canoe huffing softly. Like the flying fish they swam in pairs,
hundreds of them headed southeast, each pair rising to breathe in
passing. The haze thickened.

Hiiaka! So, you're now a wife of Tangaroa. I hope he's given you
many children. Do any resemble me, an ordinary man, or do they
all have fins and swallow air from the sea? I've loved you all these
years, many years. . . the number escapes me. Half the lifetime of
someone who grows old and whose body aches. Do you remember

the firelight? Are there fires where you are, ovens of stones in the ground under the sea? I'll eat a lot of baked fish, unless the fishes are your friends. We'll laugh, as before. Are you cold, Hiiaka? Can you recall the rain on your skin?

The sea is so calm, the whole sky lies mirrored in its face. The constellations, they're all in front of me, Rangi's universe. One stone will send it reeling. The black circles I make will stride outward, lifting the canoe and breaking up the stars' reflections. If I see demons while awake I am mad, but if I see them in sleep I'm merely dreaming. Which is this? The stone is tied to my ankle: the sail hangs motionless. Here I stand Tangaroa, another maker of silver bubbles. Come squeeze my chest.

Cantor's Theorem

I begin this brief discourse with sadness and regret. Let my words be a warning to others that the study of biodiversity is doomed. Near a remote village in the South China Sea the Man of the Caves shattered my dream of an academic career, exploding a myth about units of diversity and the categories devised to contain them.

We knew nothing about the Man of the Caves until arriving at the village, a cluster of dilapidated huts on a beach of blinding white sand. Behind the village rises a green mountain, its peak submerged in a cloud forest. We came after many arduous days and nights during which every aspect of life aboard the banca had become routine, even the shared food bowl and shitting over the gunnels. In addition to myself there were my assistants Fernando and Felino and three local fisherman. I had come to this remote place to collect unusual specimens that live among submerged rocks and corals. These animals are of interest only to taxonomists: scientists who describe, name, and classify Earth's biota as a means of assessing its variety.

Our visit to the caves was purely coincidental. Before coming here we had camped for several days on a tiny spit of land, living on fish, rice, and a few fruits and vegetables purchased from residents of nearby islands. Our work there had ended and it was time to move on. Late one afternoon in May we loaded the banca and motored an hour to an unnamed coastal village squatting behind a fetid mud flat bordered by mangroves. A festival was in progress and the entire population was drunk. Our supplies were low, and continuing on was impossible. Bed would again be the deck.

Early next morning we went ashore for a breakfast of bread, mangoes, bananas, hard-boiled eggs, and coffee. Rain had fallen in the night and cleared the air of dust, revealing fierce orange amaryllis that illuminated the edge of the forest. After waking the proprietor of a tiny store to buy supplies we began the day-long journey around the southern shore.

Upon arriving at our destination that evening we rented a small hut with a raised wood floor, its roof and walls made of palm leaves. There were no screens, but the cots had mosquito netting. We drank warm beer at a two-table cantina with an Australian who worked for a survey company. He told us about the Man of the Caves. This Australian lived in a tent at the edge of the village. In front of his tent was a very tall antenna.

Breakfast was moldy bread and lukewarm coffee. I visited the latrine afterward, a communal hut consisting of two walls and a floor with a hole in the middle. Toilet paper? An old edition of *El Nacional*. Someone had worked the crossword puzzle in ink and without error.

Later we collected specimens along a coral reef just beyond the village harbor. Rain stung our bare shoulders, and the clouds covering the top of the mountain descended to sea level. That evening we moved to a hut beside the underground river that emerges from caves inside the green mountain and empties into the sea.

After making more collections the next morning we decided on a whim to visit this subterranean river. At its mouth we hired two canoes paddled by guides. Fernando and Felino rode in one, I in the other. Our guides placed lanterns in the bows, and we entered the gigantic caverns. At our approach numerous bats dropped from the ceiling into flight, shrieking fiercely before disappearing inside the mountain. I went ashore at some of the small alluvial beaches to collect burrowing crabs. It was at the last of these that the Man of the Caves stepped out of the blackness and beckoned me to him. Our guides, speaking a local dialect, had mentioned him to Fernando and Felino, and Fernando had translated for me. Between their tales and the Australian's the man's sudden appearance was not unexpected.

His face was invisible, but he seemed of medium height and build. He had long white hair and a white beard, and he wore a robe that I learned later had been fashioned out of spider silk. The material was not woven but had a matted appearance, as if handfuls of cobwebs had been collected and pressed together. He invited me to sit with him on a damp boulder. Both of us were barefoot.

"Are you comfortable?" he asked, shyly it seemed.

"Yes," I replied, "except for having my toes buried in bat shit."

"You get used to it," he said. "Oddly, my life-long case of athlete's foot has gone into remission since I took up living in bat caves."

"When was that?" I asked.

The Man of the Caves leaned back and clasped his hands behind his neck. "I'm not entirely certain. Five years ago, although it might be ten. One's circadian clock resets itself under conditions of perpetual darkness. Anyway, time isn't important."

"What are you doing here?"

"What am I doing here?" He seemed momentarily confused. "I'm not certain of that either. Once I was a scientist, a taxonomist, actually. I studied bats."

"I'm a taxonomist too," I said.

The Man of the Caves sighed as if suddenly being told unpleasant news. "Now I remember why I'm here," he said in a voice barely louder than a whisper. "I needed a quiet place to think while attempting to disprove Cantor's theorem. Unless I succeed no taxonomist's effort will ever be valid. Our life's work will have been for nothing."

I was stunned. I had already planned species descriptions of the organisms now preserved in small vials aboard the banca. With their publication tenure was almost assured. Perhaps a monograph and eventually a full professorship would follow. What I was hearing could not be true. "What's Cantor's theorem?" I asked weakly.

"Oh, probably nothing," my companion answered with a wave of his hand. His voice had an uncertain quality. "It's just something

I've been working on for the past five years. Or is it ten? Anyhow, it's of interest mainly to taxonomists."

"I'm a taxonomist," I reminded him.

He looked in my direction and I felt his gaze for the first time. "So you are," he said. "Sorry, but when you don't see people for years on end you sort of forget they have faces. Then you forget they have minds or feelings. And finally, you forget they exist. Please accept my apology." We shook hands. His felt like the golem's.

"Would you mind explaining Cantor's theorem?" I asked the Man of the Caves.

"Not at all," he replied. "It works like this. Cantor was a nineteenth-century mathematician who demonstrated that there are more categories of things of any given kind than things of that kind. From my angle of interest, Cantor's theorem says that more categories of bats exist than species of bats. 'How can such a thing be?' you ask. But it's true." The Man of the Caves looked down at his feet and wiggled his toes around in the muck.

"I don't understand," I said.

His head turned toward me. "Think of it this way. Every attempt to correlate things of a first kind to things of a second kind—call the second kind species if you like—can never account for all the things of the first kind. No correlation of bat categories with bats ever accommodates all possible categories of bats. There'll always be some categories left over."

He stood and shouted, "It's enough to drive a taxonomist crazy!" As if on cue, thousands of bats dropped from the ceiling and dipped around our heads, shrieking and peppering us with turds. Fortunately I was wearing a hat. My companion was bare-headed, but seemed not to notice.

"It sounds too paradoxical to be true," I said.

"It is paradoxical," he agreed, "but it's also true. Forget for the moment that species might be individuals and think of them simply as categories along with everything else. Now suppose you devise a simple taxonomy into which every species of bat potentially fits. You could have fishing bats, vampire bats, fruit bats, brown bats—even one-winged bats, weak-kneed bats, or bats newly arrived from Hell. Any kind of bat imaginable. And what's the result? In the end you still have bats that aren't members of the category with which they're correlated. These leftover bats then form their own category, even if that category is empty, and it's a category of bats not correlated with any kind of bat. There's the paradox: if a correlation existed, then a particular bat would fit into this category if—and only if—it didn't. In other words, for every category of things, even infinite categories, there exists a larger category." He sat down heavily and sighed.

"Which category is that?" I asked.

"Why, the category of its subcategories."

Clearly my career was over. "What should I do?" I asked.

The Man of the Caves shrugged and spread his arms in a gesture of tired desperation. "Go home, resign your position at the university, and take up another line of work." Then he added, "But don't think about returning here. This cave is occupied, and there aren't enough mushrooms for two." He stood and walked away from me, vanishing into a crevice. His passing left a squishy sound.

As the Man of the Caves advised, I returned to the banca immediately and emptied my samples overboard. Then I ordered a puzzled Fernando and a curious Felino to take me to the city where I could catch a flight home. That was, how long ago? Five years? Ten? Time matters to ecologists and physiologists, but to taxonomists the passing of time has little relevance. Organisms evolve slowly. The differences we record are products of millions of years. No, time isn't a factor, although filling in our own can be tedious, not to mention risky.

The stationery on which these words are typed bears the letterhead of an accounting company in an inland city. My title is Trainee instead of Assistant Professor, and my place of business is neither a tropical ocean nor a laboratory but a tepid room cluttered with desks and computers and file cabinets, a place where public nakedness is an open shirt collar.

I must go now. My lunch break has ended, and this afternoon will be devoted to a seminar titled Survival in the Field. We accountants (including trainees) go into the "field" to perform audits. Sometimes the hotel bed is only queen-size or the wine list is poor. Taxis occasionally don't stop when we hail them. How is one to survive? These and other "field" problems will form the basis of lively give-and-take discussions.

The other trainees are young; they whisper. They wash their hands before playing office grab-ass. The pallor of their collective skins is evidence of a positive tropism activated by fluorescent light. Their taxonomies comprise balance sheets, depreciation schedules, deferred payments—things of a kind arranged to fit into categories of things of a kind. I presently lack courage to tell my superiors about Cantor's theorem. When I do—as eventually I must—the accounting profession will become extinct. Are there categories to contain such insidious cowardice as mine, and if so, is the category into which I fit an empty one?